HOOFING IT

At first it had only been a spot on the horizon, but now it was nearer, and it had become long and narrow, rising out of the hard, hot earth, enveloping everything under it, moving slowly toward Slocum with a rumbling roar.

Then, all at once, near it a rifle cracked and then another, followed by a third. As Slocum watched he saw the cloud of dust explode into a hundred parts, re-forming almost instantly into an enormous mass, a thundering avalanche, the sound of which increased with every pounding hoof.

Slocum didn't hesitate. His heels dug into his horse's flanks, and it leapt forward to meet the oncoming mass of bovine fear and fury.

Through the dust Slocum could see the longhorns, more than two thousand stampeding beasts, crazy with sudden terror. Their thundering hooves made the earth tremble beneath them.

He rode in a direct line for the center of the stampede, the dust choking him, burning his eyes, cutting into his face like tiny blades. . . .

OTHER BOOKS BY JAKE LOGAN

JAKE LOGAN

SLOCUM AND THE DEATH COUNCIL

B

BERKLEY BOOKS, NEW YORK

SLOCUM AND THE DEATH COUNCIL

A Berkley Book / published by arrangement with
the author

PRINTING HISTORY
Berkley edition / December 1991

ISBN: 0-425-13081-9

A BERKLEY BOOK® TM 757,375
Berkley Books are published by The Berkley Publishing Group,
200 Madison Avenue, New York, New York 10016.
The name "BERKLEY" and the "B" logo
are trademarks belonging to Berkley Publishing Corporation.

PRINTED IN THE UNITED STATES OF AMERICA

10 9 8 7 6 5 4 3 2 1

1

The tall man with the broad shoulders and the cat-green eyes stood very still and looked down at the dead man. He had dismounted his Appaloosa pony and held one rein loosely in his left hand. His other hand was not far from the Colt .45 that rode at his left hip in its cross-draw holster.

The Appaloosa's bridle jingled as the horse shook his head at some deerflies and bent to crop the buffalo grass that ran from the bottom of the long draw down to the willows that stood at the edge of the river.

Overhead, an eagle swept the sky, and from somewhere in the breaks came the bark of a coyote. But John Slocum remained motionless, studying the dead man, and the ground near him. At the same time he was listening to his surroundings, alert to the slightest hint that he was not alone. It was clear that the body had not been dead for very long.

The man was lying facedown and had been shot in the back. A neat hole right between the shoulder blades bore evidence to this.

Slocum knelt in order to examine the corpse. He saw that the man had been shot with a rifle, from not too great a distance. But who was it? And for an instant Slocum found himself considering that it might be the man he'd been coming to Eagle Pass to see. He was just getting ready to turn the body over when he felt a change in the atmosphere, and at the same time the Appaloosa lifted his head and nickered.

In the next second Slocum had thrown himself away from where he was hunkered by the dead man and rolled and dived into the protection of a stout stand of bullberry bushes.

He was absolutely still now, his six-gun in his fist, as he lay on his belly, with his eyes on the dead man and also taking in as much of his surroundings as he was able.

Silence. The Appaloosa shook his head against the intruding deerflies, then bent to rub his long nose against a foreleg.

The man who now stepped into the clearing was short, stocky, and he carried a cut-down shotgun poised for action. Slocum watched him kneel by the dead man and check to make sure he was dead. A quick look at the bullet hole, a rough pull at the corpse's shoulder, and then he put down the shotgun and rolled the body over so that it was facing the sky.

The stocky man whistled between his teeth, and Slocum wondered if that was a sign of recognition. The man was carrying a shotgun, so it wasn't likely he had done the killing. Not likely, but also not impossible, was Slocum's next thought as the man stood up.

Slocum stepped out into the clearing. "Somebody you know?" he asked, holstering his six-gun.

The short man nodded. He had small eyes, and a jaw like a bull. His shoulders were massive; he gave the impression of being as broad as he was tall. He was still holding the shotgun.

"It's the sheriff," he said. "And who are you?" As he spoke the shotgun moved.

But Slocum's hand streaked and he had the stocky man covered with the Colt.

"You're fast," the short man said.

"When necessary. Who are you, and what are you doing here?"

"The name is Hagers. Who the hell are you?"

"You know this feller, you say?" Slocum replied with another question, watching the stocky man closely. He was not at all prepared for the other man's answer.

"That's Sheriff Clyde Mulrooney."

"Was." Slocum corrected, to cover his reaction.

The stocky man nodded in acknowledgement of the fine distinction. "Yeah. Was."

Slocum walked over and looked down at the dead man, holstering his gun, his eyes taking in the tin star on the rough dark blue shirt.

"Maloney, huh?" He intentionally said the name wrong, playing for time.

"Mulrooney," the short man corrected, squinting at Slocum.

"Clyde—"

"That's what I said." His eyes were hard on Slocum.

But Slocum kept himself away from it. "Clyde Mulrooney," he repeated, but not really saying it to the other man. It was Clyde all right; even though he'd grown a beard. Dammit again! Coming too late, by so narrow a margin!

And too late he caught the Appaloosa bringing up his head and snorting.

"Throw up yer hands!" And that voice directly behind him meant right now.

Slocum had his eyes on Hagers, who was watching him, but also obviously seeing past him, to the voice that had given the order, though Hagers made no move to raise his hands.

"Up!"

Slowly Slocum lifted his hands, his eyes on Hagers who still held his hands at his sides.

"Now, turn round."

He did so, and faced a heavyset man who must have been in his forties. He had graying hair at the temples and a scar running across his large nose.

"You're under arrest."

"What for?"

"For the murder of Clyde Mulrooney, sheriff of Cole County, which includes the town of Eagle Pass."

"Mister, I don't care what it includes. And put down that gun. I didn't shoot anybody."

"I do believe you did!" The hard eyes were popping right out of his knobby head. "I says you did. An' I be the sheriff's deppity."

"What did I shoot him with?"

The grin that faced him now had all the elements of wolf in it. Without another word, the man with the gun nodded at Hagers. "Hagers there is deppity, too. He's witness. Exceptin' now he'll be sheriff, since you shot and killed Mulrooney."

"But what with? He was shot with a rifle. All I've got on me is this Colt." And he pointed his thumb at his holstered six-gun.

The man who claimed to be a deputy nodded at Hagers again. With his whole body fully alert, Slocum watched the stocky man walk over to the Appaloosa and draw the Winchester out of its saddle scabbard.

"You're not claiming I shot him with the Winchester!"

"Shit, that's what you done!"

"It hasn't been fired."

The deputy shrugged, and looked again at Hagers, lifting his eyebrows, pursing his thick lips, and with a grin in his eyes.

Hagers pointed the rifle at the ground and pulled the trigger. The report spooked the Appaloosa who gave a jump, throwing his head, but then settled.

"It's bin fired now," Hagers said.

The winter had been hard, and it seemed spring had taken a long time coming to the high country north of the Powder River. But now summer was here, and the land breathed in a fresh way. The light was different and in the long draws of the high mountains the grass was lush, green, over four inches, and the grazing was good. It would fatten a lot of beeves.

This day was—like so many others—absolutely clear. Only the bright sun was in the sky, sitting there like a burning wafer. And when the occasional eagle or jay flew on its way through the great basin of blue it only emphasized the stillness and the marvelous absence of the unnecessary.

Now, in the late afternoon the long, lonely rays of light reached quietly over the town, touching the wooden buildings, the dusty streets, the new cattle pens down at the railhead. And as evening came lamps were lit, and the air, reaching an even finer freshness, carried an expectancy, as though making ready for something about to happen.

In an upstairs room at the Everlasting Saloon four men sat around a bare wooden table. The air was filled with cigar smoke, the grainy smell of chewing tobacco, and the heady odor of whiskey and beer. On the table lay a random deck of cards, still in discard, for the game had ended. Somebody had won, others had lost. Nobody seemed to mind—it was a casual game—for their attention was someplace else than on the pasteboards that lay in such disorder. A stiff silence had filled the room, more potent than the heavy tobacco clouds, sharper than the musky odor of liquor. It was the kind of silence that held men together, even when they disagreed with one another.

At this point the single door of the room opened and a fifth man entered. He was tall, brooding, with a drooping, tobacco-stained mustache, yellow galluses supporting baggy pants, and the stub of a cigar clenched in his teeth.

"Well, Homer?" These words came from the heavyset man in the striped shirt who was sitting under a wide, white Stetson hat with a crisp brim. A man of some fifty years, most of those years seeming to be in his belly.

"Not a sign. He plumb disappeared." The words came out in a gravelly voice, spoken around the cigar stub in Homer's mouth, though everyone got the message.

"Gone!" This from another man at the big table, his tone matching his wide eyes, as though he couldn't believe what he was saying.

"Plumb gone," said Homer.

"You sent someone—?"

"I sent myself to his place, after me and Billy looked for anything we might find in his office."

"And what at his house?" asked the man with the wide eyes. He was a chunky man with a blue birthmark across his forehead. His name was Ludlow Franks, and he was the town banker. People often said he carried the smell of money wherever he went.

Homer Content replied to this question with a shrug, and turned his attention again to the man wearing the crisp white Stetson hat. This was Calvin Phobis, lawyer. Cal played the part of a legal guardian with enthusiasm. His calling was always emphasized in the way he addressed people. That is to say, he generally spoke to a man as though he was about to arrest him. In this manner, Cal Phobis reminded people that indeed there was law in Eagle Pass and environs. Some people were reminded of its intricacies, others of its escape routes. In any event, Cal Phobis was seen as an individual to deal with, and no man to try to shortchange.

Nor was Homer Content a man to attempt to manipulate. Homer, tall, with that drooping mustache that seemed to need those yellow galluses in some way or other, ran the Enterprise House, Eagle Pass's lone hotel. Homer was a man who more often than not voiced his views on how the town ought to be run, and these acerbic comments had earned him the reputation of being difficult.

On the other hand, Doc Linus, the gent seated closest to the window, opined that it wasn't that Homer was difficult, but that he should have followed the way of the cloth, for he seemed well suited with that critical, picking way about him; and besides, he loved hearing himself talk.

Doc, on the other hand, was famous as a man of few, but generally potent words. Doc could cut a man to size with that funny smile on his face, and when the fellow got outside, he'd discover he had his head in his hands. Or, as Doc sometimes put it more colorfully, he found his head up his ass.

Finally, there was the slender man softly drumming his fingers on the table. Arthur Glendenning owned Glendenning's Dry Goods Emporium. No one would have taken Mr. Glendenning for a man of the soil or the grim-faced frontier. Arthur's specialty was in slickering the greenhorns, the dudes, even the gambling folk. He looked so innocent, so disarming, so quiet, always in the background somehow, until the moment of kill. Then, as somebody—probably Doc Linus—had put it, Arthur was there to hand you back your head; or again, resorting to his more pungent and essential lingo—your balls.

Obviously, Arthur Glendenning's interests were not circumscribed by the boundaries of his store. No one knew where Arthur had come from—no one tried to find out—but he evidently had been educated; maybe he even read books. But—as everyone knew—with the talent he had for dealing, it didn't matter where a man came from. What was important was where he went.

And Arthur Glendenning, a man with an occasional English accent, understood this better than any of his fellows. At any rate, he had a sizeable bank account to show for his point of view.

"Gentlemen, without a lawman in Eagle Pass we are in a tight, and that's for sure." It was Arthur Glendenning who said these words.

"I think we have figured that out," Doc Linus said

dryly. "The point is, what the bunch of us are going to do about it."

There was just a tinge of color in Glendenning's white cheeks as he looked down at his very clean hands, lying in front of him on the table. "I appreciate your—uh—rather succinct observation, Linus. You always speak well, but the point is what *are* we going to do? Or is it more important to see what we are up against? That is to say—who?"

"Couldn't agree more," mumbled Doc, his nose disappearing into his glass of whiskey.

A tight silence fell and suddenly, without anything more than a clearing of his throat, Cal Phobis reached for the whiskey bottle and began pouring. The gesture appeared to relax the group; at any rate, it took their attention for a moment from the difficulty they were facing.

"Should we send out a posse?" Ludlow Franks asked. "He could have had an accident. It happens."

"We've got Hagers covering up around the North Fork, and he's taken Gillis with him. I thought it better to send them in pairs," Glendenning said. "Or, rather, I asked Homer to handle it since I was tied up."

Doc Linus cut a sharp glance at Homer Content then. "Those two didn't mind you ordering them?"

"They did not!" The words came snapping back as Homer's big face darkened.

Doc grinned, leaning back in his chair, his legs stretched out as he crossed his ankles. "Good to hear that the law is finally recognizing this concerned citizen's group."

"The proposed council," said Cal Phobis. "Let's put it that way."

"Why don't we just say council?" Ludlow Franks

said. "There isn't going to be anyone running against us. Except—uh—possibly Doc here." And he arched one eyebrow, grinning so that the quality and aim of his humor was not out front; and it could be taken either way.

Doc was used to such peccadilloes, as he called them. He didn't mind. And in fact, he didn't wish to be on any council. He'd only agreed to go along with the others because of his status as a physician in the town. After all, he knew just about everybody, and so his allegiance, even if laced with cynicism, was of value. It added to the image of solidarity. For if the proposed council could claim the loyalty of such a public doubter of political and social values as Doc Linus, then it simply showed that they did indeed represent a true cross section of view and opinion.

"But we've got to find Mulrooney," insisted Glendenning, bringing his palm down smartly on the table and leaning on it.

"Sheriff Mulrooney—if I may call him that—is, as we see, essential to our plan." It was Dr. Sophocles Linus speaking, leaning back in his chair with his arm bent so that his hand was grasping the back of his neck as his eyes wandered across the ceiling of the room.

"I would like to know why you insist on referring to Mulrooney in that shitty way, Linus," said Glendenning. "I'm referring to your 'if I may call him that' phrase, and other times when you seem to feel that the sheriff is less than perfect."

"Your 'sheriff,' who you have snookered into office and then regretted it, is no man to be trusted. He's too damn smart for our good. The trouble is he knows damn well when to come in out of the rain. Oh, I know—I know—" He held up a restraining palm as Glendenning and two others tried to interrupt. "I know he was the one you figured you could handle. But you see he's walked out the minute you took your eyes off him. I'll give anybody odds he's got something going on his own; and I'd bet a nugget or two it ain't something to make this jolly little group happy." He chuckled. "Wouldn't surprise me if Mulrooney up and decided to run against you." He waggled his long forefinger at them, chuckling.

At that point, almost by signal, there came a knock at the door.

"Come!" snapped Cal Phobis, and the brim of his white hat seemed to shake with indignation. "Who the hell is it!" These last words were low, but no less heard by the assemblage as Deputy Honus Hagers entered.

"We are in session, Hagers," Glendenning said. "What is it?"

"Have you found the sheriff?" Phobis cut in, glaring at Glendenning.

"He's dead."

This statement, which came out of Deputy Hagers as though he was simply announcing the time of day, brought a couple of whistles from the assorted company, a muttered curse from Ludlow Franks, and a knowing smile from Doc, into whose mind the picture of the late sheriff appeared as he was when he'd last seen him, standing on the top of a ladder while painting the front of his office on Main Street, looking down and saying, "I want to come and see you, Sophe, got somethin' in my belly—guts ain't right." And Sophocles Linus remembered this, he was certain, because no one had called him Sophe since he'd been in medical school. It was always Doc. And he had liked hearing his old nickname again.

Strange, he reflected now, because he hadn't known Mulrooney all that long. But then Doc was a sentimental old bastard.

"What happened?" Ludlow Franks asked. "And shut the door." He cut his eye quickly to Glendenning to be ready to stem any objection from that raspy quarter, but the Englishman was silent.

Hagers stepped farther into the room and shut the door behind him.

"He's dead," he repeated.

"Jesus!" Doc's whisper could be heard clearly by all. "I do believe we heard you the first time," he added, slightly louder.

"How?" Phobis asked patiently.

"Shot in the back. Rifle."

"Dry-gulched, by damn!" Homer Content's hoarse whisper brought a dimension to the event that had been lacking.

Doc Linus picked up on this, and thought how strange it was, for they had hardly known Mulrooney. None of them had been close.

"He had family, did he?" Doc asked. "I believe he did," he went on, answering his own question and trying to remember a woman, a young boy. He wasn't sure. "Is someone bringing in the body?" he asked.

"The body's at the icehouse. The killer's in jail." Hagers was speaking to Glendenning more than to Linus.

Doc said, "I'll take a look at him."

"He'll need more than that, Doc," said Ludlow Franks, rubbing his fingers nervously over the blue birthmark on his forehead; a familiar habit.

"Who shot him?" Phobis asked, slapping his question in fast in order to get ahead of Glendenning.

"Feller me an' my new deppity picked up and arrested," Hagers said.

"He got a name?" Homer Content asked.

Hagers shifted his weight and said, "Feller said his name was Slocum. John Slocum."

In the silence that followed this statement, Dr. Sophocles Linus's forehead lifted into a series of wrinkles as he stared at Deputy Hagers. And a low, almost silent whistle escaped his pursed lips.

Cal Phobis was the first to speak. "We'll try him, but it sounds like there ain't much sense in it. You say you saw him, did yeh?"

"Caught him red-handed," Hagers said. "Winchester .44-40 it was."

"Good enough, then. We'll hang the son of a bitch likely in the morning," Cal Phobis said, and he lifted his glass. "A drink to the late departed, gentlemen." And there was the suspicion of a smile on his face, at the corners of his eyes and mouth.

At any rate, it was noticed by the observant Doc Linus, who now said, "But there has to be a trial, gentlemen."

"Man was caught red-handed, didn't you hear?" said Content.

"I heard. But there has to be a trial."

Glendenning put down his glass and turned his full attention to Linus.

"Tell me, Doctor, why are you so adamant about a trial? Of course, we'll have a trial. We are all law-abiding citizens, and Eagle Pass—God bless us!—is an absolutely law-abiding town! So there's no need to insist like that!"

"I am insisting, Arthur. I am very much insisting."

"But why?"

To Linus, Glendenning's shining smile looked as though it had been attached to his face.

"I am insisting because I am not at all sure that John Slocum shot Sheriff Mulrooney."

An astounded silence fell like a clap of thunder; in fact, those were the very words Doc Linus used to describe the situation as he went over it later in his mind, and still later as he told it to his closest friend, Consuelo.

But right now, an answer was required from him. His four companions and Deputy Hagers were looking at him with a rather bloodthirsty expectancy, though none had actually spoken.

"Why?" said Homer Content. "Do you know this man? Slocum, is it? Tom Slocum. I never heard of him."

"I have. And it is John Slocum," Linus said. "The point is, I fear we could really get ourselves in a mess if we just hang him. Slocum is not a nobody. He has friends around."

"Yourself?" Glendenning was cocking an eye at him, appraising, and yes, sneering. There was a definite sneer, Doc noticed, in the son of a bitch's face.

It was Phobis who smoothed it. "Sure. You're right, Linus. We were acting too quickly, I see. Justice and all that. But we must stick with the law. Have a trial. Best, as soon as possible." He looked around at the gathered faces. "He is right, gents. It would not look good if this feller Slocum had friends, I mean in places that could put a burr under our saddle. And it should be easy enough to prove it in a fair trial. After all, what the hell, Hagers here and what's-his-name, his deputy, saw him. So, it shouldn't take long. But we ought to do it legal. Set the right way for the town to see they got law-abidin' people runnin' things. Now listen; one thing we do got to do is start thinkin' who could handle the sheriff's job. I mean that is something we ought to tend to right now."

A silence settled over them all now, while a chair creaked as Cal Phobis shifted his weight.

Suddenly, Doc Linus started to laugh.

"What the hell's so damn funny?" snorted Homer Content.

"It is not anything so funny," Doc said calmly. "It is too sad and dumb to be funny. But if we've got the John Slocum I am thinking of locked up in the town jail, then we've buggered our best bet for a sheriff."

"But maybe he ain't the same!" Hagers said, and he looked at Glendenning.

Doc, watching closely, caught the very faint shake of Glendenning's head, while holding his eyes sharp on the deputy. So that was it.

Glendenning dismissed Deputy Hagers, and the five men began to discuss this new twist to their plans.

2

The Eagle Pass jail consisted of a huge log—actually a felled spruce—to which the prisoner was chained. The log itself was attached with Manila rope to a stall inside the barn in back of the sheriff's office.

Slocum's two captors, Deputies Hagers and Gillis, had escorted him into town, riding his Appaloosa but with his hands tied together around his saddle horn.

"You'll stay here till yer trial," Hagers had informed him. " 'Less you excape, and then we'll kill you and you'll stay in Eagle Pass forever."

Both Hagers and Gillis grinned at this broad humor.

Slocum said, "I was a friend of Clyde Mulrooney, and like I already told you, I was coming here to Eagle Pass to visit him. Mulrooney had a lot of friends, and not just around here."

"That ain't gonna do you no good," Hagers said.

"Nobody's going to believe I shot him."

"You are looking at two witnesses."

Slocum got nowhere with the argument, as he had predicted. But he had decided to give it a try, anyway.

It was now almost dark in the big barn. And by the time the sun was down he could only make out vague shapes. He wondered if they were going to bring him something to eat, or whether they would just plan on killing him as he "tried to escape." In any event, he knew he had no time to waste.

But his prison, unique as it was, was absolutely foolproof. There was no way he could get out of that chain. No way. But he remained calm, knowing that the best thing was to keep a sharp attention, and also to husband his strength. There just had to be a way. And somehow he knew there would be.

They had stabled the Appaloosa at the other end of the barn, and there was no way he could get over there and try to use the animal's muscle in some way or other that could help him. About the only thing he could do was work at his manacles, trying to slip his hands out. But they were on tight, and already his wrists were cut and bruised. Nor could he budge the eyebolt that was holding the chain to the log. What about the lock? Could he pick it? For some strange reason they had not taken his pocketknife. But it was no help, and he almost broke the blade.

He lay back, exhausted. His leg hurt; his fingers were cut, and he could tell they were bleeding. His knuckles were bruised from trying to move the log.

He recalled Clyde Mulrooney, an older man, and a good one. A good lawman. The bastards!

But he had the pocketknife. Funny how they'd overlooked it. Maybe on purpose? So that later they could claim he'd attacked them, and so were justified in killing him? Maybe something like that.

Finally, he decided that the best thing to do was to rest, for he was going to need every bit of his strength.

That was about the only thing that was clear. His way of escape sure wasn't.

Now it was pitch dark in the barn, and even the sounds of revelry from the saloon nearby had died down. It had to be late, he told himself.

He dozed, not allowing himself to fall into sleep; but simply to rest, to refresh himself somehow for the struggle ahead. For by now he knew damn well there wasn't going to be any such nonsense as "a trial." Not with a bunch that murdered the local sheriff and pinned the blame on a passing stranger. He had not really wanted to reason with them the way he had; telling them he was a friend of Clyde's, that he was coming to Eagle Pass in response to a letter. No, he hadn't wanted to say a damn word; but he had to try what he could. Nothing, of course, had worked. It never did in situations like this one. Still, it was on the record, so to say; it was known that he was a friend of the sheriff, of the law, and whether anyone heard it or not, it had been said. And for all he knew somebody just might hear it.

Yes, now he was sure there was someone up near the door. A guard, more than likely. Ready to shoot when the moment came.

But he could not fall asleep. He must not! He wouldn't. He knew how to rest while not actually sleeping. Years on the trail had taught him. And so he rested. He waited.

And then all at once he was wide awake. Someone was there. Not the man by the door, but somebody else. He heard the Appaloosa stir in his stall. And again for maybe the twentieth time he mentally measured the distance between himself and his horse.

"Slocum—" The voice was barely more than a whisper, and someone touched his leg, then his arm.

"Slocum—"

"Yeah— Who are you?"

"Stash, friend of Mulrooney. There's a guard by the door."

"I know. That the only one?"

"I think so."

He felt the hands on his leg now, then the click of a key turning, and then the release of the manacle that had held him to the chain. He was free.

His rescuer smelled of sweat. It had taken a while to get the key to work.

"Call him over," the voice said.

Slocum waited. He had been gently rubbing the circulation back into his ankle and part of his leg.

"How long have you known Mulrooney?" he asked, moving slightly away from his rescuer, ready for an attack, should it come.

"About a year. Listen, this ain't a put-up job. Nobody's waiting to gun you, exceptin' that bugger at the door. Follow me."

"I don't know anybody named Stash," Slocum insisted.

"Stashnewicz. You know me. You know me from down in Round Rock, near the Hoodoo."

Some of it came back then.

"Let me feel your neck," Slocum said.

"Here."

He ran his fingers inside the man's collar.

"You remember the rope burns, do ya?" the man named Stash said. "You ought to, Slocum. You were the one saved my ass that day. You convinced now?"

Slocum reached out and touched his shoulder. "Let's get out of here," he said. "I'll give you a couple minutes."

He waited, listening. Then he suddenly called out, "Hey, you up there by the door. Let me outta here. Lemme loose. I'll sign a confession that I shot and killed Mulrooney, but let me loose. Anything you want, but let me loose!" And he started to yell and scream and shout, and act as though he had lost his mind.

"Shut up!" the man at the door yelled back. "God dammit! You do all your talking in the morning, either to the judge if he comes by, or if not him, then the necktie party that's just waitin' to stretch you!"

But the guard's harangue was abruptly cut off as Slocum heard the thud of the pistol barrel that was laid alongside his skull.

"I've got horses waiting in the alley in back," said Stash, coming back fast to where Slocum was rubbing his stiff leg.

"I want my guns. They're in the office."

"Hurry!"

He found them right off in the gun cabinet—the Colt and its holster and belt, and the Winchester. He didn't like leaving the Appaloosa, but it was too risky taking the time to tack up. He'd come back. He knew he was coming back.

Still, there was a surprise in store. The horses were in the back alley just as Stash had said, but there was a third horse and someone holding the three of them. A kid, it looked like, as he and Stash came running out of the office in the dark.

Without a word, the figure handed him the reins and he mounted, all in one smooth, swift movement. And they were walking their horses quickly behind the row of houses that faced Main Street. It didn't take long to get to the edge of the small town. And in a moment they would be free to let their horses run.

Stash led the way, and Slocum was right behind him. The boy who had been holding the horses was going with them, he saw.

Except that as the unknown rider drew abreast of him when they let the horses have their heads, he saw the outline of a face as the moonlight suddenly appeared, throwing its light over the whole earth.

"We'll be lucky not to be seen," said Stash as he laid his heels into his horse, and all three animals broke into a gallop. But Slocum had caught the profile of the young face riding beside him. It was a beautiful face. It was the face of a young woman.

The night air was soft and at the same time crisp against his bare face and hands as they rode swiftly to the mountains. Then, ascending more slowly to higher altitude, he could feel the change in his lungs, in his whole self that the thinner air always provoked.

It was a marvelous night; the dome of the sky was sprinkled with stars. Each moment seemed to bring new smells, a new freshness, too, and always within the unity of the sky above and the earth below their horses' feet.

Stash led the way, though on occasion they had been able to ride abreast; but now, climbing higher on the mountain trail they went single file, with Slocum bringing up the rear, the girl in the middle.

At one point when they had stopped to rest their horses, the girl introduced herself as Alison. She was Mulrooney's daughter, which Slocum had guessed when he got a closer look at her features. He judged her age to be twenty-some. He remembered Mulrooney mentioning something about family when they were down at the old Hoodoo spread. Stash apparently had tied in with Mulrooney and his outfit about a year ago, after Kate Mulrooney had up and died of the croup.

Stash had been working for the Hoodoo, too. And when he'd come upon a gang of night riders rustling some horse stock, he'd made the mistake of confronting them, resulting in a bullet in his chest and a very close shave indeed with a rope necktie. Slocum had chanced on the lynching the rustlers were trying to pull, and had rescued Stash in the nick of time. The scars on Stash's neck were still there.

Just about dawn they came to a particularly steep climb, where they dismounted and led the horses for a stretch to a flat area close up under the rimrocks. There was the log cabin Stash had told him about along the way.

Riding in through spruce and pine past a horse corral, a log barn, and a bunkhouse, they eventually reached the main cabin itself. Slocum fully appreciated the placement of Mulrooney's spread. Even in the dark and early dawn, he realized that Stash was right when he said the outfit was invisible from below.

A tall man was waiting for them in the protection of the thick timber surrounding the place. He was holding a goose gun in one hand, and seeing who the visitors were, he stood it against the side of the corral and approached them.

Now the sun was just at the tip of the horizon and light was transforming the sky.

A shepherd dog detached himself from a stack of firewood and ambled over to sniff.

The tall man said, "You be Slocum, I reckon. Clyde's friend. I'm Pete Mulrooney."

"You look like Clyde," Slocum said, remembering Clyde had mentioned a brother.

"That's what folks say. I knowed Clyde wrote you about comin' to help out."

It was then that Slocum saw the other man had a cast in one eye while there was a hardly discernible limp as he reached the corral. Putting his weight now more on one foot than the other, he reached up and rubbed his hip.

"Bronc fell on me 'bout a month back, but it's mendin'."

"That can hurt," Slocum said.

"Reckon you could get outside some hot coffee and maybe some flapjacks, it bein' 'bout that time."

"I sure could."

"Ali—"

The girl was already starting toward the cabin. "I'll have it on right now," she called over her shoulder.

She had hardly spoken as they rode and this was the most he'd heard from her. She had a soft voice. He wondered how she was taking her father's murder. He knew it was those quiet ones, those ones who made no great display, who suffered the most. She obviously had the quality that he remembered in Clyde. Though they hadn't known each other all that long, still there had been a bond. Nothing said, but something felt. The girl was like that, he could see. Alison. A nice name.

Now the sun was reaching over the rimrocks above the Quarter Circle M, and he had a clear view of the flat area that had been cleared by Mulrooney and the log cabins and barn and corral he'd built using the timber that surrounded the place. From below, the ranch was invisible. Only from the top of the rimrocks, Pete Mulrooney told him, could it be seen. And then only if you looked twice.

Now, relaxed in the Mulrooney kitchen, with the steaming cup of excellent coffee in his two hands, he observed the girl and Pete Mulrooney.

"You sure look like Clyde a good bit," Slocum said, opening up as relaxation came after their long ride, and the grim experience with his captors and the Eagle Pass jail.

"Some people have taken them for twins," Alison said, speaking directly to him for the first time since they'd arrived at the ranch.

"I'll be riding into town," Pete said. "Likely this day or no later than tomorrer."

The girl suddenly put down her coffee. "Uncle Pete, please don't go too fast about—about Dad. I mean who actually did it—" And she stopped, her eyes filling, and then she suddenly put down her coffee mug and left the room.

"It's hurtin' her bad," Pete said to Slocum. "But you know, we bin sort of expectin' it. Somethin'. Not really anything this bad. Fence cutting, like. Changing brands. Even some rough stuff. But nothing like this. Like killing—" He seemed to be looking beyond the log walls of the cabin.

"How do you mean?" Slocum asked. "How were you expecting something like that?"

"Since he got to be sheriff," Stash said, speaking for the first time. "Clyde never wanted it, but the outfits around here wanted him to take it. I dunno how he ever got past that bunch in town."

"What bunch?"

"Like the council they begun. Glendenning and Content and them others. They wanted a sheriff and they tried to get Hagers in there, but they made the mistake of askin' for a vote, and everybody wanted Clyde. He didn't want it, but he done it on account of he figgered if the people wanted him, then it was right for him to take it."

"He was certainly the right man for the job," Alison said, coming back into the room at that point. "But—" She looked away.

"Maybe not talk any more about it," Slocum suggested. "Miss, I could use some more of that great coffee."

And suddenly she was smiling at him and he felt something inside him turn over.

"I just love to hear compliments," she said.

Slocum watched her as she reached to the range and took up the coffeepot and poured. Her blue eyes were shining, and the sunlight coming through the kitchen window now shone on her dark brown hair, shooting off the morning light like magic, Slocum thought.

Pete had been sitting with his forearms on his knees, leaning forward, holding his coffee mug between his hands. Now he lifted his head, squinting at the three who were sitting with him, and reaching up, pushed the brim of his Stetson hat back so he had a better look. "We'll get him," he said. "Or them. Whoever."

"Do you know who did it?" Slocum said. "I didn't see who pulled the trigger. It looked like it was those two, or one of them, but I don't know for sure."

"I am talking about the man who ordered it," Pete said, looking at Slocum from under the wide brim, with one eye closed like he was squinting at something in the distance. "I'll find the son of a bitch."

"Uncle—"

"Sorry. Didn't mean to talk like that in front of you, Ali."

"It's all right. I was talking about something else."

"I know—"

"No, I don't think you do. I'm saying there's been enough of this kind of thing around here. Which was why folks wanted Dad to be lawman in the first place. But we don't need more."

"You mean you want them—!"

But she cut him off. "No, I don't want them to get off scot-free. But I want them brought to justice. Not more killing."

Slocum felt something stir deeply inside him as he watched her facing up to her uncle.

"He's my brother, and mind you, we got to get aholt of Clyde out of that icehouse and plant him."

"I know. But let's find out the facts. Let's find out who is actually to blame."

"You know who's to blame. Content and Franks and them others what's calling themselves the representatives of the people."

A silence fell, and then Stash said, his tone idle, yet trying to smooth the atmosphere, "Reckon you'll be riding on, eh, Slocum. I mean now that—"

"No," Slocum said, interrupting him. "I'll hang around a bit. Maybe right in town there. Clyde asked me in on this thing, so I agreed. I wouldn't feel right leaving him now. I mean, if that's all right with you-all."

Pete Mulrooney gave a nod at that. And Slocum saw the smile come back into Alison's face.

"We'll get 'em," Pete said. "We'll get 'em."

"But with the law," Alison insisted. "Please, Uncle Pete. Just killing people isn't going to help anything. It'll only make things worse."

Slocum pushed his hat back on his head. "Don't want to break in on family," he said. "But she is right, Pete."

Pete was holding his eyes steadily on his niece, not saying anything for the moment. And then he sniffed, nodded, it seemed in token of what Slocum had pointed out.

"Exceptin' Clyde—he was my brother."

Alison had been looking down at her hands lying in her lap. Without raising her eyes, she spoke.

"And he was my father." She raised her head and looked at Pete through her tears.

That night Slocum and Pete slipped back into town and brought the body out to the ranch. No one had been at the icehouse, except an old-timer who was more drunk than asleep, sitting outside the log cabin with his bottle. Pete said he was one of Clyde's former deputies. They had no trouble taking the body out and tying it to the packhorse they'd brought along. They were back at the ranch by dawn, and within the hour had lowered Clyde into the grave that Stash had dug while they were away.

"It'll stay unmarked till this mess is done with," Pete said, as he closed the prayer book from which he'd read. "By golly," he said then as the sun rose, lighting the whole of the wide country, "Clyde'll have a good view of the valley." And they all went back into the house and had a drink of Old Overholt to Clyde Mulrooney.

The five men who comprised the Eagle Pass Council, as they called themselves, reconvened early the next morning at the Everlasting Saloon to plan John Slocum's trial.

No sooner had they seated themselves than there came a sudden loud ruckus outside in the corridor that ran the length of the building, and off which the girls who plied their wares at the Everlasting Saloon maintained their cribs where they received their customers.

Homer Content stepped to the door to investigate, but just as he was reaching for the knob, there came a loud knocking.

The door burst open as Homer pulled back on it, and a man with a tin star on his shirt almost fell into the room. He was out of breath.

"Hagers! Gillis! What'n hell you doin' here! You're s'posed to be guardin' the prisoner, God dammit!"

"He done excaped!"

"Come in! Come in!" barked Glendenning. "And for God sakes shut that door!"

"How did he escape!" Glendenning demanded furiously.

"We had him chained to a log and I left Gillis to guard him all night. Someone got the jump on him and sprung Slocum. My idiot deputy couldn't mind a graveyard without the corpses excaping!" replied Hagers miserably, glaring at Gillis.

Hagers's rage at Gillis, his deputy, had spent him. He was exhausted, speechless with the problem of Gillis's stupidity, incompetence, inability even to walk across the street without sliding in horseshit and likely breaking his leg! He said so. He said so at the top of his voice, until Glendenning and the others told him to shut up.

"The point is what have you done about getting this man back?" said Ludlow Franks, glaring at both Hagers and Gillis. "Hell, he must've left some kind of trail! Does he come from around here? Who the hell is he, anyway, and why did he shoot and kill Mulrooney! And God dammit, how the hell did your prisoner escape? For Christ sake, next thing we hear will be that your prisoner took Mulrooney with him!"

This outrageous sally brought a roar of laughter from the group, though the embattled Hagers and Gillis could only manage rather sick smiles.

Suddenly Glendenning said, "Hagers, get some men together, including your deputy here—Gills, or whatever his name is."

"Gillis," said Hagers.

"And find your prisoner. We want him back here by tomorrow morning. Early! To stand trial. Now then, hop to it!" His words came crackling out of his thin mouth and he followed Hagers and his deputy to the door, as though sweeping them out of the office. Then he closed the door smartly behind them.

"Now then," he said, turning back to the group. "Let us continue with our meeting. I suggest that we call a public meeting to announce some of our new appointments."

"But what about this man Slocum?" Homer Content asked. "And the trial."

"We can't try the bird who has flown until he either returns to the nest, which he is surely not likely to do, or we are able to locate him. And I don't hold much hope for that."

But before anyone else could say anything, there was another knock at the door.

"God dammit!" snapped Glendenning. "There are more interruptions here than at a woman's tea party, for Christ sake. Who the hell is it now!"

Doc Linus could hardly contain his laughter at the way things were going all widdershins. And he totally failed to contain it when the door opened and to everyone's amazement it turned out to be Hagers, who had only a moment before left.

Hagers was red in the face, and his hands were twitching. Doc took note, however, of the man's courage—or was it his stupidity?—in returning to the fray.

"Forgot somethin'—"

The five members of the self-appointed council regarded him in abrasive silence. Stone would have been more friendly, Doc was thinking, and almost felt a little sorry for the struggling deputy, who quite obviously had simply been following orders. Linus assumed the orders had come from Glendenning, arriving at this notion as a result of the swift look he'd caught passing between the two men the day before.

"Well, what is it?" Glendenning's words fell like ice into the doorway, keeping the man there, not allowing him to take a step into the room.

Doc watched Hagers's Adam's apple pump in his throat. "Forgot to tell you somethin' that feller said, Slocum."

Silence, while the Adam's apple pumped again.

"He said as how he knowed Clyde Mulrooney; why he'd come to this part of the country in the first place. Mulrooney wrote him, askin' him to come. That is what he said, so help me Jesus!" And Hagers stood there. He was all but shaking, and to the point where Doc Linus almost felt sorry for him.

"So what?" said Franks.

Hagers's formerly ruddy face was now white. "I dunno," he said, almost stammering as he faced that wall of negativity. Save for Linus, they were all standing around the table now, in a semicircle as though ready to wipe him out, Doc thought.

"I dunno," Hagers repeated. "Just thought I better tell you."

The room had frozen now as they stood there regarding the deputy who had dropped this astonishing news into their meeting.

After a long moment, Homer Content said, "He say anything else? Slocum, I mean."

Hagers nodded, eager for the chance to move the scene along to some place less tense, less dangerous.

"He said as how he'd come out to visit with Clyde Mulrooney; how he'd known him down to the Z Bar T outfit near the Hoodoo Range south of Tensleep some while back."

Doc Linus was still sitting in his chair, leaning back now and even enjoying himself. Doc was a man who was interested in people and the things that happened to them, and he found the present scene highly entertaining. By God, he was thinking, by God! And he was recalling a quote from Shakespeare: "What fools these mortals be."

He grinned, feeling superior, but not in a mean way. He was a man who found it difficult to really dislike anybody. It had often seemed to him—knowing this about himself—that he had therefore chosen the right profession. Or—and this thought interested him too—the right profession had chosen him.

He took his watch out of his waistcoat pocket. Good enough. It was getting along to that time of day when he would be meeting the lovely creature who drove him into maniacal passion with a single look, a brief touch. It was a good life, he decided. A very good life. What a pity these fools he had to deal with had to take everything so bloody seriously!

In an earlier time, a thousand head of beef cattle would be considered a pretty big herd. But it wasn't long before the herds began to be made up of five, six thousand head. Of course, the number of men making up the trail crew was geared to the size of the herd. The rule was one or two drovers to a hundred head of cattle. And those trail hands were chosen with extreme care. Each cowboy needed as many as two to six horses. Then, besides the herders, there was a trail boss, a cook, two horse wranglers who handled the extra horses, several wagons, pack mules to pack along provisions, and plenty of firearms, saddles, lariats, short-handled whips, blankets and other bedding, slickers, and the regular clothing and personal belongings of the riders. All of this was just the minimum of what made up the outfit.

Slocum knew it well. Trail driving was no holiday. It was brutally hard work and it was lonely. And by the time those lonely cow waddies got anywhere near the town that was their designated shipping point for the cattle, they were itching to tear the place wide open. It seemed more often than not that they did just that.

Eagle Pass, one of the northernmost and newest shipping points, was no exception. And Skintown, on the other side of the railroad tracks—and thus more or less isolated from the proper side of town—was not really unusual. People said it was what it was, "only just more so."

The buildings in that peppery community comprised a baker's dozen of roughly built wooden houses, including two dance halls. One of these establishments was owned and operated by a gentleman known as Three-Finger Harold; the other was under the counseling and direction of Two-Ton Priscilla Handles.

These edifices were some twenty-five yards apart from each other, and other buildings surrounded them;

small cribs where the employees plied their wares.

The ground near the buildings was almost bare. The grass had been worn away long ago by the feet of numerous patrons. At any hour of the day or night—including the Sabbath—music and the sounds of dancing could be heard from at least one of the the two houses.

Each house had a well-stocked bar, and it was a rule that the dancers patronize the mahogany at the end of each set of dances. Each bar, of course, enjoyed more than the patronage of just the dancers. There were almost constant spectators who showed up eager to witness firsthand the wicked pleasures of the wicked West.

Men in all stages of alcoholic joy or sorrow crossed between the houses, sometimes seeking a change of music, but more usually on the prowl for a fresh partner. In a corner of each hall there was the inevitable gaming table, and a dozen girls were on duty in each dance house.

Here, then, was heaven for the Texas cowboy, especially since Eagle Pass had opened its arms to embrace the beef traffic to the big cities of the East. Somebody, very likely Doc Linus, had remarked that this was no less than paradise for the boys from "Takes-Us," as they called home. They could be seen everywhere, all over Eagle Pass, but especially in Skintown.

No doubt about it, John Slocum agreed as he wandered about taking in the sights. The drovers were every place he looked, on the streets, in the saloons, the gambling halls, and for certain in Skintown's raunchy establishments. Meanwhile, on the surrounding prairie, thousands of longhorns grazed.

He had ridden in that morning with Stash; Pete and Alison holding down the ranch. Slocum had made it plain that he wanted to stay with them, as they had suggested, but he also insisted that he would require a free hand. And he had made the two men agree that there would be no shooting unless under extreme provocation. They had agreed. They saw the sense in his caution.

"You know they can wipe us out like swatting a deerfly," he told them. "So we'll play it easy."

"But they can catch you if you go back into town," Alison had pointed out, her face peaked with concern; which Slocum had to admit, pleased him.

"That will be the risk I take," he said. "Sooner or later they'll come looking for me here. And that would involve you and Pete."

"Let 'em come," the lanky man said, squinting his game eye at the ceiling, then looking directly at Slocum. "But I see your point. Meanwhile, I'll be about. My leg is 'bout ready, an' I'm looking for the opportunity to pop a couple of those no-goods."

And so Slocum had ridden into town, reluctant to leave the girl, but feeling better when he reminded himself that just before leaving, Pete had told him that he would be with her night and day.

It was just turning into evening now as he stood outside Two-Ton Priscilla Handles's establishment and lit a cigar. The sun was almost at the horizon, casting long shadows over the town, as the air received a twinge of coolness, turning Slocum's thoughts to the pleasures of the building he was about to enter; yet, at the same time, this very thought in turn reminded him that he was in town on business. Scouting, listening, looking for anything out of the way, exposing himself just enough so that his presence would be known, circulating among those who had been so interested in him and had had him jailed. Offering himself as a decoy. For he had Stash shadowing him, at a distance. And he had confidence in that man. A man you've saved from a hanging is a man you've maybe got to feel confidence in, he told himself ruefully. For Stash was a good man; a man of few words. At the same time, John Slocum was no dreamer. Early on he had learned one very important thing about men, and women, too. This was that the only thing you could trust in people, the one aspect of the human being's character that was always predictable, was that a human being was simply not predictable. This view of the human condition had saved him a lot of trouble over the years.

It suddenly grew darker and some faint stars began to appear overhead. A light breeze stirred, bringing the rich odor of a herd of longhorns nearby on the surrounding prairie.

Stepping inside Two-Ton's blazing establishment, he immediately caught the wild jangle of the upright piano, the violins, and banjo, in accompaniment with the scraping of heavy boots, while now and again above the screeching of the straining instruments rose the "do-si-do" of the nimble caller. At this moment it was Two-Ton herself assuming that role, and it was one of her favorites. She held the room as though it was in her hand. An enormous woman, a veritable pachyderm, Slocum saw, yet with a relaxed randomness of movement, voice, and gesture that gave life to the orchestra and the dancers. What he noticed especially was that the lady had the good sense not to try to hide her enormous dimensions, but rather made use of her great size. Her laugh was as huge as she was, and was equally magnetic. Her voice bellowed the words to accompany the music. She even danced, solo, on tiny feet. It made him

wonder whether she would trip herself and come a
cropper. But there wasn't even the hint of such a
calamity. She was everything she needed to be for
the occasion, and when the round ended, he applauded
louder than anyone near him. At the same time, he had
given that extra applause for another purpose, too, that
of attracting some attention to himself. For he knew,
as he'd told Stash and the two Mulrooneys, that the
best way for him to find something out was to make
himself a target.

Watching the scene, Slocum found himself com-
paring the place to Annie Jack's palatial quarters in
Denver, which was the last house of pleasure he'd
visited. Annie, it was said, ran the fanciest cathouse
in the wild West, and maybe, some people allowed,
in the whole western world, Europe not being of any
account in such figuring. Annie had beautiful girls
and furnishings that would bruise the purse of a rich
man: a huge mahogany staircase with a carved banister,
exquisite cut-glass mirrors, thick red Brussels carpets,
and crystal chandeliers. No, he could see right off that
Two-Ton Priscilla's wasn't in the same money class
as Annie Jack's, but there was something here that the
Denver mecca was lacking. And of course, he knew, it
was Two-Ton. He had swiftly realized that she was a
person who could take a bare barn and bring it to life
simply by walking into it.

And by golly, there the lady was. Later, he was
to recall his encounter with this fabled individual as
memorable; indeed, the moment required definition in
quite another realm. Two-Ton was definitely not ordi-
nary.

She seated herself at a table with the world spread
before her, though the most immediate properties were

her deck of cards, her drink, and the handsome, obviously expensive cigar that she was so clearly enjoying. Her head was covered with slicked-down black hair, and she smelled heavily of pomade. Her facial features were all large: large eyes, large, broad nose, heavy lips with much lipstick, while her great cheeks were heavily rouged. She wore heavy gold earrings hanging from long lobes. As she sat there, ensconced behind the big, round table with the bright green baize top, she looked like a statue, something that would require assistance to move; like a monument, Slocum decided. Her shoulders were covered with black lace, and a folded fan lay on the table close at hand in case of a sudden attack of perspiration, which Slocum realized she was concerned over, for she kept dabbing at her cheeks, the wings of her great nose, her neck, jowels, and the corners of her scarlet mouth, her bronze eyes with their enormous, false lashes; a tiny, even petite lace hanky daintily gripped between a huge, sausage-shaped finger and thumb.

Slocum had a sudden tremendous urge to laugh as he looked at her, and this impulse was all at once swallowed—as though by itself, not by him—and he felt the backs of his eyes sting, just for a second, as he suddenly, in an incredible moment *saw* her.

The instant passed, but he knew that he would never forget it. He knew too that he did not ever want to forget it. It was not often, he well knew, when you saw a person inside, as it were, seeing clean and whole. Yes, the child; the buried diamond.

However, at the same time—as he well knew—you had to deal with the adult, the tiger often enough. And he could see right off that Two-Ton Priscilla was no pussycat.

"Try your luck at three-card monte, sir?" The crackling voice drove Slocum instantly into the world of the jungle as one huge, bejeweled hand reached for her glass of whiskey and the other removed the cigar from her scarlet mouth.

"Wouldn't mind," Slocum said with a grin, stepping over to the vacant chair in front of Two-Ton. "Try a hand or two, though I'm a mite out of practice."

"You don't look outta practice to me, buster." This was said hard as a cold deck, and was not meant as any pleasantry, Slocum realized right off. He wanted to grin. By golly, he liked her, though he knew he wouldn't trust her as far as he could throw her. She was handling that deck like she'd given birth to it.

"Pick the ace," Two-Ton said without looking up, as her big shadowed eyes followed her own hands switching the cards with lightning speed. "Now you sees it, now you doesn't."

Flashing the ace again, she turned it over so that only the backs of the three cards showed, all the time switching the cards. "Follow the ace. Where is the little fucker?"

Slocum took his time. Her hands were moving faster than those of any dealer he'd ever seen.

All at once the hands slowed. The massive figure was almost still.

"Here is the ace," she said, and flipped the card over so he could see the face, then placed it facedown. "Follow it, now." She moved the cards slowly. Her hands stopped.

"Which is it?"

"The ace?"

"I wasn't talkin' about yer Aunt Nellie!"

"That one." He pointed.

"Wrong!" And she turned the card over. It was the seven of hearts.

Slocum chuckled pleasantly as Two-Ton collected the cards and built her pack, then slapped it down onto the tabletop.

"Mister, you 'pear to me 'bout like a stud hoss trying to fool a mare he ain't got a hard-on!"

"Why, Miss—"

"The name is Priscilla. An' I ain't no miss. I have had—count 'em—four husbands. Not one of 'em worth a cupful of cold piss. I spotted you right off. You know the cards. What are you doin' here? Figurin' you'll cut yerself in on a little business? Well, sir, forget it!"

"I'm just looking things over."

"Girls?"

"I don't pay for it."

"Huh!" Her enormous bronze orbs rolled up and down his chest. "Ain't you the one!"

"Maybe we could talk a spell."

"My time is money, mister." She paused, her eyes again rolling up and down his chest, his hands, his face. "You're that one that got took for shooting Mulrooney, ain't you."

He nodded.

"What the hell you doin' in town then?"

"I didn't shoot him, and they know it. I'm here to take a look about."

"They already know you're here."

"Who does?"

She didn't answer that. She simply sat there behind the table, her fat forearms lying on the green baize top, her eyes taking in more of him than just his features. Those eyes were like fingers, probing him.

"Thought somebody like you might help me," Slocum said.

"I ain't in the helpin' business, mister. That's all I can say to you, 'specially with that gent yonder by the dice table cutting his eye this way more than every so often."

"Got'cha."

She was shaking her head slowly, and very definitely from side to side. And he knew that was for the benefit of the man watching.

"Isn't there any way you can help me? I just need an opening, a little crack so that I've got something to work with. For instance, if somebody wanted Clyde Mulrooney to be sheriff of Eagle Pass, then why did they also kill him?"

"Do you know for a fact it's the same ones wanted him for sheriff what shot him?"

"Can you tell me?"

"If I could, I wouldn't." She reached for the cards, her eyes dropping as she fanned the pack open.

Her voice was low, almost beyond his hearing, as she spoke. It was impossible to see her lips move.

"Take a room at the Longhorn Cottage. Come back here in a couple hours an' ask for Nellie."

She was dealing herself solitaire as he rose. The man by the dice table followed with his eyes as Slocum left. He could feel those eyes like a touch on his back as he went through the swinging doors.

3

"Eagle Pass, hell!" was the comment of one old-timer that reached Slocum's ears as, two hours later, he started to reenter the Premier Saloon Drinking and Eating Emporium, which was owned and operated by Two-Ton Priscilla Handles. "It's Eagle Shit is what I says!"

The old timer came reeling back through the swinging doors, almost bumping into Slocum as he swayed and stumbled, totally out of control, to finally fall with a loud thump onto the raised board sidewalk just outside. Looking back over the top of the batwings, Slocum saw that this adventurer was sitting up, in his rumpled, ragged clothing, laughing with the tears streaming down his face.

"First bath old Clem has had I bet in a month of Wednesdays!"

The comment brought surprise to the face of John Slocum—and interest in the man who had spoken—for he'd never heard the remark made except with the designated word being Sunday. And for a split second he watched the back of the receding figure, still looking over the top of the swinging doors. There was, in fact, something strangely familiar about that back and that walk, but he couldn't place it. In a moment, somebody brushed past him, mumbling some words of irritation, and he turned back to the saloon and walked to the bar.

The next thing he noticed was that Two-Ton Priscilla was nowhere in sight. Yet she had told him to return in a couple of hours and to ask for somebody named Nellie.

"I'm looking for someone named Nellie," he said to the bartender, who placed a glass and a bottle of whiskey before him.

"That's me," a voice said directly behind him.

But Slocum checked himself and didn't turn around immediately. Instead, he picked up the blond hair, the bare shoulders, and the turned-up nose in the mirror.

"Well, you sure look like her," he said, speaking to the mirror. And he lifted his glass of whiskey in a toast and took a light swallow.

"I reckon I do look like her," the reflection said. "Since that has been my name for the last—hmmm"— she screwed up her face as though giving the question serious thought, and then suddenly opened into a wide smile—"for the last about hour and a half. Well, I'll be dingdonged if that ain't a pretty good piece of time for a beautiful example of feminine intelligence, beauty, and uh—well, real honest-to-God good looks and— an'—"

"And a pretty lively way of looking at this here world, I'd allow," Slocum said with a big grin as he turned around.

"I seem to have heard of you someplace, miss." He screwed up his face as though in desperate thought. "Spokane, was it? No—no. Maybe Denver?" He shook his head. "Cheyenne? Yeah!" He beamed. "It was Cheyenne!"

"Never bin there in my whole entire life. But I will tell you where it was."

"Where?"

"Aw shucks. I forgot!"

And they both burst into wild laughter.

Obviously, the bartender knew her, for he had poured a drink and placed it within easy reach.

She grinned at Slocum. "My usual. I take it for my nerves."

"Nerves?" He stared at her. "Miss, you don't look to me like you've got a nerve in your whole body." And he let his eyes rove approvingly over her hips, which were the most provocative he'd seen in a good while, to her bust, which seemed to be bursting the seams of her black satin dress, and ending up with her eyes, her earlobes, and then her lips, which were full, slightly parted, and obviously waiting to be kissed.

Slocum obliged.

"That was just what I needed," she said.

"Me, too."

"You look to me like you're looking for somebody named Nellie. I saw you come in and I said to myself, that feller looks like a feller lookin' for a gal name of Nellie."

"You said right."

"Me, I been looking for a feller name of Slocum." Suddenly she held up the palm of her hand to stop his retort. "Don't tell me. I can guess. Let's see. It's Otis Slocum. No. No, it isn't Otis. Robert? No." His eyes, meanwhile, were feeding on the cleft between her two handsomely large breasts.

"I like your eyes," he said.

"Do you—"

"I have always liked blue eyes."

"They're only blue in the daytime."

"There's no daylight in here!"

"But the eyes go by what's outside. For instance, at night—it still looks the same in the barroom here day or night—in the night, they turn black."

"Interesting," he sniffed, "if true."

"There's a way to find out. Stick around."

He was suddenly serious. "I was told to look you up. Do you know why?"

"I was told to look you up. Do you know why?"

"I see."

And then all at once she became serious. "How would you like to lie down and discuss this serious matter?"

"Where?" His erection was driving like a fence post into his trouser leg. And as she turned to reach for her drink, her hand brushed it. Slocum thought he was going to come right then and there.

"Sorry," she said, seriously.

"I liked it."

"So did I. But it wasn't on purpose."

"Shucks. I thought it was," he said, grinning.

"I can think of something we can both do on purpose," she said.

"Have you got a room upstairs?"

She nodded.

"But you better know right off, I never pay for it."

"You weren't asked to pay for it." She stuck her tongue out and added, "What I've got all the money in the world couldn't buy. Well, maybe all could. But I think you catch my drift."

They had finished their drinks and were all paid up and had started toward the stairs that led up to the balcony where the girls' rooms were.

"Not up there," Slocum said, as he turned toward the swinging doors.

"I wasn't aiming for upstairs, Mr. Slocum."

He was surprised at that. "Where then?"

"You tell me. Don't you have some place where you're staying?"

"Good enough," he said, still surprised. As they stepped out into the street, he said, "Don't you—"

"I am not part of the establishment, if that's what you're asking, Mr. Slocum."

And all at once he saw her differently. She had put a coat on to cover her bare shoulders, and in the daylight he realized she looked quite different.

It was only a short walk to the Longhorn Cottage. He gave a curt nod to the desk clerk as they entered, and seeing that he had no messages, he led the way up to his room.

When they were inside, he shut the door and locked it.

"You afraid someone will come in?" she said, sitting down on the edge of the bed.

"I like privacy."

"Well, I must say I agree with that."

And there it was again, something in her tone of voice, in her choice of words.

"Tell me who you are," he said.

"Why, I'm Nellie. I told you."

He was shaking his head. "That may be your name, but I want to know who you are. Really."

For just a split second she looked shocked. Or at any rate, he realized his question had thrown her. But she recovered immediately.

"I think I could best tell you what I'm not."

"I'm listening."

She was sitting on the very edge of the bed, with her knees together, though not clamped, he noted, and with her hands lying loosely on her lap. Yes. She was definitely different.

"To begin with, I'm not a Pinkerton."

"That's a big relief."

"I'm not working for the stock growers."

"Another good point."

"I—well, I can say I'm not working for anyone, particularly."

"I could go with that, except what about Two-Ton Priscilla?"

"We're friends." She was looking at him, watching for his reaction. "Not close, but still, like sisters under the skin."

"Somehow you don't seem—" He stopped, searching for the word he wanted.

"We don't seem to be in the same league. That it?"

"Yes and no. On the other hand, I do believe Two-Ton's a good bit different than she lets on."

"The whore with the heart of gold?"

"Not so simple," he insisted. "There are people in the world who have really learned it the hard way. I mean, there are some who've really had it tough and have survived."

"You're saying Priscilla is one of those."

He nodded. Then he said, "And so are you." And as he spoke those words, he wasn't sure but he thought he saw a tear in each eye. When she suddenly dropped her head, looking down at her hands in her lap, he knew he had seen correctly.

"I think I know what you mean," she said. And when she raised her head, her eyes were clear. "Priscilla has been a good friend. I don't happen to be one of her—uh—staff, if that's the right word. But I'm not churchy, either."

"Thank God," he said with a grin.

She was looking at him as though studying him. "You know, you're a thoughtful man. You—" She looked past him and then looked down again at her hands, speaking now with her head bowed. "In many ways you remind me of Clyde."

"I know," Slocum said, and watched her surprise.

"You knew! You knew about me and Clyde!"

"I figured it out. No, he never said anything about you in his letter."

"But then, how could you know? Priscilla—"

He was shaking his head. "No. No. Priscilla said nothing, didn't even hint at anything."

"Then, how—?"

"Well, let's say Clyde and me—we're a bit alike. Or, anyway, were. So you talked to me and all like you sort of already knew me."

"You mean, like I was at ease with you, relaxed and all that?"

He nodded. "Something like that. So it wasn't too hard to guess something, well—like I did."

They were silent a moment.

Then she said, "I'm glad."

"So am I," Slocum said. "Now, let's see, where were we?"

He watched the color slipping into her face.

"Well, not so very long ago, you kissed me."

"That's right. And we got sort of interrupted."

He sat down on the bed beside her and put his arm around her shoulders. Suddenly she turned to him and buried her face against his chest.

They said nothing. They sat there like that and he began to feel her sobbing, and his arm encircled her even more.

"Let it out," he said gently. "Let it all out."

"Are you asleep?" he asked, feeling her body relax more with his arm around her.

She murmured something, as though only half awake. He couldn't make out what it was, but his arm was aching, for they'd been huddled on the bed for quite a while.

He took his arm away, and she clung to him and the next thing he knew they were lying down on the bed side by side.

"Why not sleep a bit. I think you're pretty wrung out," he said softly, now withdrawing his arm.

"Are you going away?" she murmured.

"Wasn't fixin' to," he said. "You?"

"Uh-uh—"

Almost without realizing what he was doing, he pressed closer to her and felt his erection spring to action between her parted legs.

She slipped her arm up and around him as he reached down her back and felt her buttocks through her clothing: soft, yet firm, resilient and welcoming as she spread her legs more apart.

Then they were undressing, still lying down, slowly removing their own and each other's clothing until that moment when they were each naked, with his erection hard between her straddling thighs. Her hands moved slowly down his back now and found his naked buttocks, which were already undulating as his member stroked into her wet fur. Then she reached down, gripped it in her fist and guided it into her vagina.

"My God, it's big! You're so big!"

"Is it hurting?"

"I love it! Oh God, I love it!"

And he was on his elbows and knees with her legs spread wide as he rode his cock up high and deep into her pumping orifice.

"My God," she gasped. "Oh God, it's wonderful! Oh, how wonderful you are! Give it to me. Please, give it to me!"

And Slocum did. He gave her every pumping inch and every squirting drop of come as they exploded together, still thrashing, grinding, pumping, gasping, until the final exquisite instant.

Then they lay there, supine, joyous and devoted to whatever it was that had brought them together in such a fashion.

"You're so good," she whispered.

"It takes two," he replied.

"You drive me out of my mind!"

"I only wish to drive you out of your pants," he countered, tickling her ear with his tongue.

Now, with her middle finger she was teasing just under the head of his limp organ; which almost instantly sprang to full rigidity.

"It's beautiful," she said, and leaning away from him a little, she looked down at it. "My God, what a thing!"

"That's a pretty nice thing you've got," he said, stroking her wet slit, and running his fingers through her bush.

"It loves what you're doing."

"My cock loves what you're doing to him," he said as her fist pumped up and down, sliding on his wetness, now tickling the little slit at its head with her thumb until he thought he would go mad.

Now she had turned around with her back to him, and reaching down through her legs grabbed his member and began to ride on top of it. Then she was on her hands and knees and rubbing the head of it into her damp fur. ·

"I want it from this way," she said.

"Me too. God, me too." And he mounted her doggie fashion, riding her, with her buttocks high in the air, while he held and squeezed a teat in each hand. And came.

After which they lay there while he caressed her teats, her nipples, which were large and pink and even seemed to him to be flaming from the joy of his sucking and chewing and fingering. Until again they couldn't stand it and this time she went down on him and sucked him deep, way down her throat, with her tongue fluttering the whole length of his bulging cock. She meanwhile had lifted her leg across his body so that her soaking vagina was in his face and he buried his tongue into her as deep as it would go.

She was gasping, almost crying out with the great ecstasy of it, begging him to come or something— really, just begging. But he righted her, down on her back, and mounted her high and deep and with full authority now as he rode her bucking buttocks to the ultimate coming.

Inscribed within a handsome picture frame on the wall of Dr. Sophocles Linus's office was the fabled proverb of the early Spanish settlers of California. This poetic nutshell read as follows:

De medico, poeta, y loco,
Todos tenemos un poco.

Of the doctor, the poet, and the insane,
All of us have a little.

Doc liked to quote it. For how true it was. For anyone to head out to the western frontier, it was said that he had to have something of the poet, he was certain to be somewhat crazy, and he had to be at least part doctor.

Right now, Doc was sitting in his armchair behind his desk, thinking just that, wondering how he'd ever ended up with the strange bunch who called themselves the Eagle Pass Council. Not that he was against councils per se, but why himself?

A man of sixty now, he was still vigorous sexually, and thank God, plus thanks to Racing Bear the Lakota medicine man who had prescribed the exact herbs for the condition that he had once feared and was now laughing at.

Doc had been through it all, learning the tough way; through the action; the long, endless hours on the trail when he'd ridden his horse for miles in order to deliver a baby or to set a cowpuncher's broken leg or to relieve the aching bladder of an old man who couldn't pass water, making a catheter out of a willow branch. For, more often than not, you had to make do with what crude materials were at hand.

Broken bones, the croup, pulled muscles, appendicitis, the shakes and terrors, with always the specter of that "disease beyond my practice"—death—to deal with, death and the survivors.

He was reflecting on it now as he looked around the handsome office; the first stable practice he'd had since coming West. And he was a legitimate doctor; not some "medical assistant" who had come West and taken on the title. For the hoaxers were everywhere with their patent medicines and magic cure-alls for cholera, burns, swelled joints, ringworm, frosted feet, boils, indigestion, not to forget venereal disease. And he had ridden to help his patients as much as fifty miles with the thermometer at forty below in the hinterlands of wild and dangerous country; keeping too the midnight vigil for countless squalling, newborn babes in sod shacks and in freezing mining camps. Like his true brothers, the few-and-far-between medicos who truly shouldered their work, Sophocles Linus had earned his place.

He realized this, but he never bragged about it. He was a quiet man with a quiet humor who loved to read Shakespeare.

There was a knock at the door, just at the precise and difficult moment that he was trying to recall a verse from the sonnets. And for a moment he was irritated. Another patient? Or that same old Agrifer Helmholz who had nothing at all the matter with him medically, yet was an ambulatory box of endless complaints.

But no. Though the knocking was not forceful, nevertheless he could tell it was female. And suddenly his heart bounded.

And it was her. Consuelo Virgilian Andamamander, the most gorgeous creature he'd laid eyes on since— since? Well, since ever. He knew it was her by the knock.

He sprung from his chair, kicking the spittoon as he did so and hurting his toe, for he had taken his boots off in order to rest his feet. But he didn't care. Love, of course—and he didn't need Shakespeare to tell him this—resolved all difficulties. Though he also knew from past experience that it had a good score in creating them, too.

The great thing about the lovely creature who entered his office now was the fact that she was not yet thirty. He couldn't believe it. He was a good thirty years her senior. But by God—and thanks not only to God but to Racing Bear—he was able to drench himself, as well as his eager partner, in nightly delight that as far as he was concerned, was beyond all reason, beyond even madness.

"Come in, come in!" He felt he was chirping like a bird, but he didn't care. He was so glad to see her.

"Consuelo, my dear! Sit right here."

"But it's your seat, my dear."

"No. I insist." And he pulled up another chair, one with a straight back and waved her into the armchair he had just vacated.

She was an olive-skinned beauty with black hair combed close to her head, large, dark eyes, a high, clear forehead, and a bust she simply could not hide, with the rest of her—so Doc put it—to match.

"What brings this great event to me?" he asked.

She was sitting on the edge of her chair now, with her fingers laced together around her two knees, looking even younger than her young years.

"Dear, you asked me to keep my eyes and ears open in regard to certain matters."

"Yes, those people in the restaurant. While you're waiting on table; yes, just as we spoke about two, three days back."

"Sophie—"

"Sophe," he corrected her, as usual. It was part of a little joke they shared about strange names.

But she was serious, even though she'd forgotten to be for a moment. "Sophe, those men came. They had dinner."

"Today?" He was sitting up suddenly, his interest caught, eager for something that would break the deadlock of his thinking on the situation with the council, the approaching Texas herd that was due almost any day now, and the question of support for his medical practice. He was in need of money—as usual—but even more in need of certain supplies and equipment, all of which were costly. At the same time, being in the political position he was in, ostensibly supporting Glendenning and the others, he felt the need to be right on the edge of what was happening, not to be caught with his pants down, to put it bluntly.

"The man—the one—" She stopped, holding her hand to her forehead. "Ah yes, the one called Arthur."

"Glendenning," he said.

"That's the one. With the big teeth. Anyhow, he did most of the talking. He talked like an Englishman."

"He generally does. Who else was there?"

"A big man with a big mustache."

"Homer."

"And another man with a blue mark on his forehead. And a man with a red face and a white hat that he kept on all the time."

"Those two are Ludlow Franks and Cal Phobis." He sniffed. "Funny they didn't ask me along."

"You would have been there? They said your name."

"Oh yes? What did they say?"

"They said you weren't there."

"Jesus—"

"One of them said that, the one with the hat. And then the English one said, something like you would come next time."

"I hope you didn't let on you were listening."

"I was careful. But, as you know, some of them eat their dinner there almost every, well not every day, but maybe three times a week; and not necessarily together. Well, you've been there yourself."

"I know. That's why I asked you to listen in. What else did you catch?"

"They are expecting Texas cattle. They spoke about a railroad. I didn't get much of that talk. And they said the name Slocum and they spoke of Sheriff Mulrooney."

"So, what did they say?" He had risen and gone to his desk and returned with a bottle and two glasses. Setting them down, he crossed the room and locked the door.

"Tell me," he said, sitting down again and pouring whiskey into each glass.

"They said it was sad about the sheriff. But they want to find the one named Slocum. I don't know why."

"But how were they when they talked about him?"

She looked puzzled. "All right." She gave a tiny shrug. "I guess they were all right. I don't know. Do you mean, were they angry or something like that?"

"Yeah. I mean, like how did their voices sound. Anger? Or excited? Something like that."

She was silent, staring into the middle distance, with her forehead wrinkled. He thought she looked delightful and at the same time he felt the need to get the conversation out of the way.

"Nothing. Nothing special that I can think of. The English one, he did say something about trying to find the man named Slocum. It was like he wanted to talk with him, maybe ask his advice. Something like that. I think. I'm not sure. But that is what I think."

And she sat there now and opened her hands and shrugged. "Not very exciting, my dear. But that's what it was."

"You say Glendenning spoke as though he wanted to get hold of the man named Slocum?"

She nodded. "Yes."

"Did he sound angry, I mean like he might want to do him harm? Anything like that?"

"No. He sounded all right. Not angry, but like he just wished to see him." She looked at him with a sudden thought forming. "Is this man Slocum somebody you know?"

"No, I don't know him, but I've heard some things about him."

"Good? Bad?"

He thought a moment. "I'd say both. Good and bad. He's a man to be reckoned with, is the point."

"Someone important."

He nodded, thinking, placing it somewhere to rest, at least for the moment.

Lifting his glass, he said, "Thank you, my dear. You did well. I appreciate it."

Her smile burst all over her face, and he thought how like a young girl she was. So easily pleased. And looking at her, he felt something touch him.

"You look so thoughtful, Sophe."

He grinned at her, and his grin was wicked. "I see that it's time for your regular medical examination."

They both laughed at their running joke. He stood up.

"The door is locked?" she asked.

"It had better be." And his eyes gleamed, then closed in utter delight as from her sitting position, she reached up and felt his erection through his pants.

4

It was Arthur Glendenning who led the discussion, as
indeed it generally was. Sophocles Linus took note of
it, leaning back in his chair, as he faced midday dinner
at the Longhorn Cottage restaurant with Glendenning,
Cal Phobis, Ludlow Franks, and Homer Content.

Glendenning had suggested a late hour, when there
would be less chance of other customers being present. And so they were alone in the dining room save
for the waitress, Consuelo, known more popularly as
Connie, who kept herself well out of earshot, much to
Sophocles Linus's amusement. He could imagine what
they would all think if they knew their waitress's real
relationship to their little group.

Glendenning ran his long finger alongside his lean
jaw and with his other hand reached for the bottle.
"Gentlemen, another round." And not waiting for a
response he started to pour into his own glass, and
then passed the bottle. While all watched, and in turn
poured their own. Doc Linus appreciated the ceremony,

being one for formality whenever it was possible on the godforsaken frontier.

All drank, and momentarily their expressions relaxed.

It was Glendenning who eased the moment; wry, caustic, even, at least for him, jovial in the situation. "Well, gents, as the cowboy said to his lady friend, we're in a tight. Eh?" And the laughter moved easily around the table. Doc, joshing with all the rest who were trying to ease their worries, found himself a whole lot more interested in the marvelous swishing sound of their waitress's skirt. Consuelo was perfect, he decided, and he was impatient for the meeting to end so that— But his thought was interrupted by Glendenning leaning onto the table and tapping his glass with a piece of cutlery.

"Gentlemen, just to review. Let's take a moment to see where we are." He paused, licked his upper lip where he had made a slight cut shaving that morning, and continued. "I have been informed that the Double Back D herd left the pike June 7. Calculating that it will take thirty-five to forty-five days to move that three thousand head at a figure of ten to a dozen miles a day, that'll make it any day you guess it."

"Any day now," somebody muttered.

"The point is, are we ready?" said Cal Phobis, taking a cigar out of his pocket and sniffing it.

"The point," said Arthur Glendenning, "is also our unfinished business. Sure, we can be ready for Dyce's herd. But what about our present, immediate business. Eh?" He reached out to take the cigar Phobis offered him and sat back in his chair, his eyes suddenly following the waitress's buttocks out of the room. Across from him Dr. Sophocles Linus glared in unabashed irritation. Fortunately, he caught himself in time and had that expression off his face when Glendenning looked his way.

"You are referring to Mulrooney," he said.

"The disappeared corpse." Homer Content sighed and stared, without realizing it, at Ludlow Franks's blue birthmark.

"Jesus," muttered Franks. "You can't have a trial without a body. Can you?" he added, looking at Glendenning.

"And without a prisoner," Glendenning said. "Boys, you keep forgetting that this man Slocum is walking around free. He's apt to get into all kinds of trouble. And that would be a pity."

"Then why don't we have him taken care of?" Content said bluntly. "I mean just roughed up a bit. Nothing terrible. You know?"

But Glendenning was holding up his hand, cautioning silence. He nodded toward the door, and Franks got up and walked over and closed it.

"Open doors have ears," Doc said with a chuckle. "That's from Shakespeare, in case you didn't know." And he chuckled to himself. Christ, he thought, what the hell am I doing here with this pack of knaves? Except, then his good sense whipped into the picture and he remembered that he, too, was one of them. "A mortal fool was he / about that glorious she . . ." And he chuckled, realizing he'd better not drink any more, at any rate, not here.

"So what can we do, gentlemen, about Mr. Slocum?"

There followed a rather long silence until finally Doc Linus said, "Nothing. We can do nothing about it, for we might easily stir a hornet's nest we will regret."

Glendenning nodded. "Mulrooney had a lot of friends in town. And we'll have big trouble on our hands if we try anything. I am very glad you see that."

"That stupid fucking Hagers," snarled Phobis.

"Best to let things settle some, is that it?" Homer Content was saying.

No one said anything to that, all allowing the ensuing silence to mark their agreement.

Finally, Content said, "Hagers needs to be watched, however. He and that Gillis, too. They could upset the cart."

"And it won't be apples that fall all over us," Doc said with a sardonic grin, tapping the ash off his cigar.

"We will keep an eye on Slocum," Glendenning said. "And on the Quarter Circle M."

"Pete Mulrooney's spread, you're saying," put in Phobis, who felt he hadn't said anything for a while. But his remark disappeared into the new silence that took over the room.

For some moments they sat, each with his own thoughts. Glendenning was watching them, and Doc was watching Glendenning. He enjoyed these meetings only for the drama of the different characters in dealing with each other. The human drama, as he called it to himself, was always interesting. And when Glendenning started to speak again, he found it was the subject he'd been waiting for.

"Let us not forget Mr. Cole Berringer," Glendenning said.

Homer Content leaned his forearms on the table. "I heerd from a man I kin trust that Cole has hired himself a couple, three fast guns."

"That don't sound too healthy for the community," Doc said dryly. "How do we see this? Is it just for protection, or is there more to it? I mean, for instance, with the Texas cattle coming in."

"You mean, Cole don't want them cutting in on the market? Something like that?" It was Phobis speaking.

Homer sniffed. "Hell, I dunno. I'm just telling it like it was told me. Cole is either expectin' trouble or lookin' for it."

"Who's bringing up that drive?" Franks asked. "Anybody know the name?"

"It's the Double Back D herd from down around Quincy," Glendenning said.

"Yeah, but who? Whose herd and who is ramrodding it?" insisted Franks.

"What're you getting at, Ludlow?" Phobis said. "You got somethin' there?"

"Well, you all oughtta know whose the Double Back D spread is," Ludlow Franks said. "That's Morgan Dyce." His eyes went around the table. "Throw your memory back a little, least a couple of you, I'd say Cal, and mebbe you, Homer."

For a moment Doc thought the silence was going to endure, but Homer Content suddenly ran his hand over his face as though remembering something.

"Jesus. Yer right, Lud. Them two were not, and I'll bet a bunch they still ain't, asshole buddies."

"What are you saying?" Glendenning cut in swiftly. "Dyce and Berringer know each other?"

The sentence seemed to glare in the room as it stunned all of them.

"By God, I recollect hearing something about a feud," Doc said suddenly sitting up in his chair. "Some kind of gunfighting. About cattle, or something, some years back. That it?" And he stared at Ludlow Franks's earnest scowl.

"Jesus!" Arthur Glendenning ran his hand along the back of his neck and shook his head as he surveyed the group sitting at the table.

"Jesus ain't gonna help us with this one," said Doc. "It's up to us."

"That's correct." Glendenning was sitting upright now, severe, with his forearms on the table, his fingertips all touching their opposite companions so that his hands and fingers made an arch. "It's up to us."

"Dammit to hell," said Phobis. "If those two start throwing lead at each other, we'll have one helluva mess in this town. And I don't just mean Dyce and Berringer, but their men. I've seen the cattle towns when they get all het up on account of some goddamn feud. They take the place apart."

"So we'll have to take the necessary precautions," Glendenning said.

"But how?" cried Homer Content. "We ain't got a sheriff. His deputies ain't worth a bottle of cold piss."

"That, of course, is something we shall take into account," Arthur Glendenning said ponderously.

"But how?" Ludlow Franks was clearly agitated. "Those cowboys are wild enough when they hit a town after trail herding, but with gunslingers to boot, we are going to have a goddamn Fourth of July cellybration we might not get to remember!"

The men at the table fell suddenly silent. It was as though they had spent themselves in their sudden antagonism to the approaching herd of longhorns and had no force left with which to cope with the disaster.

"Arthur, what do you think?" They turned to him, as they had in the past when there was trouble.

Interesting, Doc thought, how people always wanted to be led. Except, he added to himself, for those moments when they wanted to lead. But, for the most part, men wanted to be led so they could have the luxury of complaining, which, as leaders, they would have had to forgo.

He was watching Glendenning, seeing the thoughts moving through the man, like clouds crossing the sky. Glendenning was a mystery. No one knew where he had come from, though that was the way it was in the West. No one had a past. Even the names were suspect.

He continued to watch Glendenning, seeing him wrestle with the problem that so suddenly and so unexpectedly had arisen.

"We could send a rider to the army," Homer Content said. "I mean, if we really feel it could get bad. They're not so far. Fort Willoughby. A rider could make it in a day, maybe a day and a half. What d'you think?" He looked around the table, but nobody met his eye. Nobody wanted to get caught. Doc saw that.

He saw now that Glendenning had lifted his head. Apparently he had come to something.

"What do you think, Arthur?" Doc asked. "How do you see it?"

Glendenning leaned an elbow on the table and put his hand at his lips. It was a posture, Doc decided, that was equal to serious thought.

Glendenning was holding his chin now as he spoke. "It seems to me it's time for a bold stroke. Nothing else is going to work."

"Bold?" said Homer, and looked at Cal Phobis.

"You may not agree," Glendenning said, "but it might work. It is crazy enough to work. If anything can, if anything at all will." He sat there with his long thumb along the side of his jaw, and his forefinger across his chin, with his elbow on the table.

Doc Linus started to speak. "You're thinking of—"

"Slocum," Glendenning said, cutting in smoothly. "I think John Slocum is our man."

"Slocum!" The name burst simultaneously from Phobis and Content; Ludlow Franks was speechless.

Glendenning was smiling. "Yes. I do believe Mr. Slocum owes us. Wouldn't you say?"

Doc Linus was grinning along with Glendenning. It was, he told himself, a good moment. By God, a damn good moment!

At Crazy Wolf Crossing, the Double Back D herd was slowly bedding down. They had reached this small branching of the Wood River that afternoon and Morgan Dyce, ramrodding his own outfit, had ordered a halt. This happened to irritate his men who, as a result of their long and difficult drive, and also in the hallowed tradition of all trail herders, were keyed to the breaking point of roaring into town to wash themselves clean of the dusty, exhausting, brutal trail. In a word, they were all most eager to wallow in the attractions of Eagle Pass.

But Morgan Dyce, a man not to be gainsaid, saw otherwise.

He had other reasons for holding the herd than for fattening on that good feed before driving them to the loading pens. These concerns he considered even more important than the rumors of the quarantine, which he'd picked up all the way back to the Chiqmauqua River, and which had followed him all the way north.

The real reason was something quite different. All the way north he had been thinking of the message from Cole Berringer, wondering if it was on the up-and-up, or if it was a trap to settle the old score.

The boss of the Double Back D brand stood now in the evening light that was only just slipping into the sky, glancing off the manes of the horses, the cattle horns, glinting on a belt buckle here and there. He stood swing-hipped, a tin cup of coffee in his hand and a cigarette between the fingers of the same hand. The ash fell the moment he lifted the cup to take a swallow, but he paid no mind to it. He was thinking about the second message from Cole Berringer that he had received when he arrived at Crazy Wolf Crossing.

"Fixin' to storm, looks like," E. T. Crimmins, his trail boss said, coming in on his thoughts, then spitting a jet of brown tobacco juice downwind.

Morgan Dyce squinted at the sky. He was a tall man, with a body hardened by years of working with stock, chasing horse thieves and cattle rustlers, and sometimes fighting Indians.

But this was familiar country to him up north of the Powder. Fifteen years ago he'd left, fifteen years after he and Cole Berringer had nearly killed each other in a handkerchief fight with bowie knives. The law had stopped them then. The cause of the fight had been Molly Dunrood, who neither one ended up having. Some dude had taken the decision on that one. So Morg had ridden out of the country, heading south to Mexico, but laying over in Texas and starting all over. Some good while later, the news came that Molly had up and married the dude and moved East.

It had been wild chance that Morgan Dyce had found himself herding his cattle north to—of all places—Eagle Pass. He'd heard the place was an up-and-growing town. He'd figured to deliver to the new shipping point because the price was good and he needed the money. He wouldn't linger there; he'd head back down to Texas with the horse wrangler and the cook, letting the men find their own way back when they'd drunk the town dry and turned their pockets inside out.

Except there had come the note from Cole Berringer. What the hell did that old son of a bitch want now! And how had he known Dyce was bringing his herd north?

Morgan had not responded to his trail boss's observation on the weather, but simply squinted at the sky, reserving judgment for later.

Now the trail boss said, "Riders comin' in."

"Heerd 'em."

E. T. spat at a clump of sage. "Sounds to be a pair."

"That's what it is," Morgan said. "How come the outriders didn't spot 'em?"

"They did. Jellicoe tolt me an' I come to tell you, which I have bin doin' this past couple of sentences."

Morgan Dyce scratched at his stomach, just inside one of his dark yellow galluses, then scratched one of his buttocks, and finally his crotch.

He had just dumped the last of his coffee out of his tin cup when the two horsemen rounded a young stand of bullberry bushes and drew rein. Cole Berringer was the near rider; the other man Dyce had never seen before.

"You et?" he said as Berringer sat his big hammerhead bay horse looking down at him with no expression on his wide face.

"Could handle some jawbreaker," Berringer said, dismounting from the bay.

Without saying anything, his fellow rider moved off, as did E. T. Crimmins.

"You made time from the Chiqmauqua," Cole Berringer said.

"Got your message."

They were each silent while Cookie came with coffee and fresh sourdough biscuits.

"Set," Morgan said, and he squatted on his haunches by the thin fire that the wrangler had only just built.

They were squatting not far from a saddle rig, and Berringer took note of the silver conchae on it.

"What's with the quarantine?" Morgan Dyce asked.

"Nothin' to worry." Berringer had picked up a branch of sage and was drawing aimlessly in the bare ground in front of him. Then he dropped the sagebrush and took a cigar out of his shirt pocket and offered it to Dyce, who refused. Berringer bit off the end, put the cigar in his mouth and wet it, then lit. "The quarantine is no big thing," he said. "The government seen the sense in not enforcing. Shit, they'd drive all of us the hell and gone out of business."

"The hell you say." Dyce nodded a couple times. "Money is money," he observed with a tight face.

"That is so."

Each understood the other was playing poker. And why not? A man had to watch his back, too, not just the man playing the hand right in front of him.

"That leaves the marshal," Morgan Dyce said. "Is he feeling friendly to us cattle drovers?"

"Mulrooney is dead." Berringer said it cold, like he was dealing a fresh hand.

Dyce looked at him and said nothing.

" 'Pears he was dry-gulched," Cole said.

"Looks like I come visitin' at the right time," Morgan said. "Shit—" Then, "Who they got now? Anybody?"

"Nobody."

"Hunh—"

"I bin thinkin'," Cole said, his tone easy, "thinkin'

since I'd heard you was on the way north, that maybe you an' me could help get this country back into the hands of cattlemen. Get it away from the goddamn land promoters and all. You interested?

"Depends."

"I'd see there was somethin' in it for you."

"Somethin' sweet," Morgan Dyce said. "I'll study on it." Then, "How's the town?"

"The town is shook, 'specially without Mulrooney. They dunno what they want, or what they're goin' to get. The town is waiting for somebody to light the match."

Morgan Dyce took a moment with that, and he looked at the man who all these years he'd hated more than he'd ever hated anybody.

"So what you want, Berringer? You want me and my men to light that match?"

It was only a small surprise when Slocum found a message waiting for him on his return to the Longhorn Cottage and asked for his room key. And when he found out who it was from, he realized he was indeed in the middle of something. The note was signed "Your poker instructor," and it told him to come and visit that very evening.

He had caught the short man looking at him from the big armchair across the lobby, and he knew that the man was there to make sure he got the message. He was tempted for a moment to go over and deliver his reply in person, but he decided to play his cards more carefully. He knew very well how much could be lost by letting one's immediate impulse carry the day. So he ignored the person who had been sent to spy and simply pocketed the note.

He read it again when he got up to his room. Then, seeing that it was still early in the evening, he decided to take a short rest and also think through what he had learned so far.

The striking thing was that no one had tried to confront him. Nobody had taken a shot at him or picked a fight. Nor had he yet become a "permanent resident" of Eagle Pass. He knew he was being watched; the man downstairs wasn't the only one. There had been others. He was under constant surveillance. The question was, why?

He was certain that when Hagers and Gillis had arrested him for the shooting of Clyde Mulrooney, they had no idea who he was, and they had just made hay out of an opportune situation, his being on the spot at the right moment. But the boys had clearly stuck their feet in it. He felt that. It must be why whoever was running the game hadn't made a strike, but had simply kept things in a wide loop.

And then, where did Two-Ton Priscilla Handles fit in the picture? Was she in with Hagers and Gillis and the men backing them, the town council? What was the council after? Apart from law and order, what was their aim? To build Eagle Pass? The fact that they were about to become a shipping point certainly opened up a lot of opportunities for making hay, power, and maybe even making the way for someone to higher political office. This last, of course, was at the root of so many activities going on in the "opening of the frontier" and the "building of the West." And, he added to himself sardonically, in the lining of greedy pockets.

For sure, the killing of Clyde Mulrooney could have been a mistake, and now it was necessary to cover some tracks, and move in another direction. But one thing was clear, and that had to be that the fact that Slocum and Clyde had been in communication and that he'd come north to be with the sheriff—and likely "help out"—that he therefore had to be played easy-like. Gentle, though firm. For the fear would be that Clyde had let him in on information or something, at any rate, that would work to the disadvantage of those who had been behind the killing.

Well, good enough. He was sure that neither Hagers nor Gillis knew much about anything, that they were just tools. That left the question of who was running the show. Was it the town council? That was the impression that he got while speaking to Pete Mulrooney or Stash or even Alison.

Actually, he'd had the least contact with Alison. The girl had been fairly open with him, quietly friendly, but at the same time he could tell that the death of her father had hit hard, and that what conversation she had with him before he left the Quarter Circle M had been perfunctory, an effort on her part. He hadn't actually tried to get any information out of her about the town, but what he had gleaned from passing remarks and attitudes when certain people had been mentioned, fit in with the picture he was building of the principal citizens, mostly the new, temporary council. He lay on his bed, unable to sleep, not that he was trying particularly, but now he found that his thoughts were centering more on Two-Ton Priscilla and her note. He began to see that interesting individual as a sort of neutral zone between possible warring groups. It was a neutrality that very likely allowed that strange lady to deal with both sides. She had the patience of Solomon and the resourcefulness of Machiavelli, but there was no heart of gold buried in that mountain of fat. Yet, there was that brain, which he could tell was a veritable diamond. The next thing that occurred to Slocum was the possibility that Two-Ton Priscilla was playing one side against the other, and that she was planning on factoring him into her game.

Suddenly he found himself smiling at the nerve of that giant. And the admirable enterprise. A New York or Frisco banking tycoon put no more into his daily efforts of legitimate theft than someone like Two-Ton did into her nefarious capers. He had to admit that he preferred her type to the mealymouthed sanctimonious charlatans who strutted in the world of what was called "the legitimate."

Suddenly into the arena of his idle rumination came the picture of a young girl with her face drawn, her eyes red from crying, but with something else, some quality that encompassed all that grief, something more than it, something that would not let the sparkle die. She was lovely. There had been moments—instants really, for they were not even as long as moments—when he'd sensed it. A glance, a catching breath, a vibration, an aroma: atmosphere. And it had been there more strongly than any blow.

There had been these glancing-off moments, and yet something had penetrated, lasting more than things that had been taken in with serious thought and attention. She had gotten under his skin, into his blood; and for sure she was filling his loins.

He sat up, bringing his legs over the edge of the bed. There was little sense in letting his thoughts run away with him. She was obviously unavailable, and he would have to wait till her grief passed. He turned his thoughts to Nellie, a girl who was also marvelous, and moreover, available. And yet—

He changed the subject of his thoughts again. What was going to happen when the Morgan Dyce cowhands hit town? What was going to happen when Dyce and Berringer squared off? And what was the council going to do? Who was really running the town? And what was the game?

He stood up and tucked in his shirt, checked his six-gun, then sat down on the bed again and pulled on his boots.

It was then that he saw the piece of paper that had been pushed under the door. Swiftly he stepped over, turned the key in the lock, and yanked open the door. No one was there. He bent down and picked up the folded white paper. It was a printed sheet:

Have you had a physical examination lately? Why not make sure of being in the best of health? Dr. Sophocles Linus of Eagle Pass is extending his practice to include a wider public. His office is open for this special examination between noon and sunset on Monday through Friday every week.

Slocum read the notice through twice. Then he looked at the other doors that lined each side of the corridor. There wasn't a single door that revealed the white paper beneath it. Slocum knew it couldn't have been that each one had been shoved all the way under. His had not been. It was clear that his was the only notice of Dr. Sophocles Linus's offer.

He saw that the sun still had a good couple of hours to reach the western horizon, and on an impulse, he decided he'd check in with Dr. Linus before visiting

Two-Ton Priscilla, who had signed her note, "Your poker instructor."

He had heard Linus's name from Stash and Pete Mulrooney. Doc Linus. They hadn't said much, only that he was a member of the new, provisional town council, and that he always came when needed, no matter what time of the day or night. Slocum got the impression that the man was trusted. In fact, he had taken care of Clyde's wife when she was dying. It was Ali who had told him that.

He wondered how Ali was. He was wondering if it might not be a good idea to check the Quarter Circle M and see how the Mulrooneys were doing. Well, it was necessary now to keep his mind on the business at hand, namely Doc Linus, and then Two-Ton Priscilla. Life was sometimes hard, he reflected philosophically. But dammit, so was something else every so often.

5

As promised in his announcement, Doc Sophocles Linus was in his office late that afternoon when Slocum dropped by.

"I got your message," Slocum said, sizing up the wiry man who answered his knock on the door.

Doc grinned. "Just so long as you're not looking for a doctor who can cure you of mortality." And he led the way into his office.

Slocum took in the rolltop desk, the horsehair sofa, the two battered easy chairs, and the two straight-backed ones made of wood with deerskin seat covers.

"I wonder if you'd just sit there a moment while I give some milk to this cat."

"Sure." Slocum had crossed the room to look at a framed picture of two bare-knuckle fighters on the wall directly opposite Linus's desk.

"You fancy the ring, do you?" Slocum said.

"Not especially. I used to box a little, but not for a living. Aah—the prize ring and Shakespeare, an interesting match, eh?" He spoke while bending to pour milk into a saucer for a dark gray cat with luminous blue eyes.

"Can I give you a drink?" he said as he straightened up. "I mean booze, not this poison."

"No. Let's get down to what you want from me."

"Well, it's not to examine your health," Linus said, with a friendly smile. "But I did want to meet you about the episode with Clyde Mulrooney—the shooting."

He sat down, not behind his desk, but in an easy chair facing his visitor.

"You're talking to me now as a member of the town council?" Slocum asked.

"Not really. I am on the council. But I've taken it upon myself to make your acquaintance privately. See, I'd heard of you, Slocum. Here and there. Nothing specific," he added quickly, holding up his hand to allay any suspicions on his visitor's part.

Suddenly he turned to the gray cat who had left the bowl of milk and with tail straight up was marching toward the door of the office.

"What's the matter! There something the matter with the milk?" He was out of the chair and squatting by the bowl which the cat had spurned. Lifting it, he sniffed. "It's perfectly good. What's the matter with you!"

But the cat had reached the door and was now sitting on its haunches looking back at Doc.

"You want to go out? You know where you can get better milk? You ingrate!" He strode to the door and opened it, and then closed it firmly after the disappearing figure, only just missing the cat's tail as it flowed arrogantly after its owner in the nick of time.

"Idiot!" he muttered, returning to his chair. "Never satisfied. If it isn't the milk, it's the food. The other day— Well, never mind. I won't take up your valuable time. Let's get back to our conversation."

"I find the interesting thing about cats," Slocum said, "and horses, and animals in general, is that they never talk back or argue with you."

"It's undoubtedly why one refers to them as 'dumb' animals."

Slocum grinned at that. "It is interesting, too," he said, "that they live according to law and custom." He shifted in his chair. "But let's get into what you want from me."

"I'm not exactly speaking for the council now, or even as a member of it. But as a private, concerned citizen." His eyes, which had been trained on Slocum, now shifted to a spot in the ceiling. "I speak to you in confidence, Slocum. May we agree on this point before I go any further?"

"I'm listening."

"First, I want to say that I am not being disloyal to the council, speaking to you privately. I will share with them what is necessary, but I realize that if we all met you, as a group, well, we'd get nowhere and it would take forever."

"I understand," Slocum said, nodding. "You want to find out where I stand on certain issues before you bring them or me to the council."

"That's it exactly."

"So—?"

"I do believe I will indulge at this point," Doc said, reaching for a drawer in his desk and bringing out a bottle and a glass. "Change your mind?"

"Maybe later," Slocum said, still not giving anything extra to the other man.

Doc poured swiftly, returned the bottle to the desk, lifted his glass in salute, then took a healthy swig, exhaling deeply and well within range of his visitor's nose as he lowered the glass. "Aah! That's what the doctor ordered!"

"Smells great," Slocum said dryly.

"You've likely heard that there's a big cattle drive coming in. Fact, the herd's waiting just the other side of Butte Basin. I've been told it's two thousand head."

"I heard twenty-five hundred," Slocum said. "And it's Morgan Dyce himself ramrodding the outfit."

"I see you are up on things."

"Hard not to be in this town."

"Indeed!" Doc Linus took a pull at his drink. "Indeed, that is so. There's little you can hide in a small town."

"But don't you feel that those are the best places to hide things, in the small communities where everything appears to be open and clear and known?"

"I know what you mean."

"So what are we hiding here?" Slocum said. And he kept his eyes directly on Dr. Sophocles Linus.

Doc cleared his throat, reached for his glass, and drank a generous portion of whiskey.

"Jesus! But that is strong medicine!"

"You made it yourself, did you?"

"Wish I could, but no."

"You've got something going, and you want me to help you with it," Slocum said. "I'm pretty sure it involves the law, and more than likely the presence of Mr. Cole Berringer and the sudden, unexpected arrival of Mr. Morgan Dyce. Correct?"

Doc nodded. "We—the council, the five of us—have gone to a lot of trouble to handle this town, which is about to start growing—not gradually, oh no—but in leaps and bigger leaps. We have no idea where it will all end up."

"Let me ask you something."

"Shoot."

"Why are you on the council?"

"Because I was asked to be. Don't ask me why they asked me. Probably because I'm a doctor, which is sort of next to being a preacher. We don't have a preacher—at least not yet."

But Slocum was shaking his head slowly from side to side, even before Doc had finished speaking. "No. Tell me. Tell me really why."

For a moment, the other man looked nonplussed. "I really don't know what you mean."

Slocum got to his feet. "Then there isn't anything for us to talk about," he said.

"Sit down. Slocum, sit down. Please!"

He stood there looking down at the other man who was still seated.

"I'll try to tell you why. But sit down. Please, sit down. Slocum, it hasn't been easy."

"I figured that."

Doc was sitting on the edge of his chair now, with his eyes on the floor near his visitor's feet. "You know then. About me."

"I only know you're hiding something," Slocum said. "And it's got a grip on you. You're scared. I can see that. Why don't you tell me what it is. It can't be the worst thing in the world." He was looking squarely at Linus now. "Or can it?"

A silence fell now that was like a bond between them, and Slocum felt suddenly sorry for the man sitting there staring into his past.

"There was—someone. She was close. We were close." The words came slowly. But then they seemed to grow stronger as the story took form. "She was going to have a baby. Mine. But, well, we couldn't. I don't need to go into why not. Yes I can. It would have killed her to have it. I knew that. But the doctor she went to said no. He said she had to have it. And there were her parents. And—" He stopped, controlling himself as his staring eyes faced into the past.

"So you helped her not have it. And—"

"They blamed me for—for killing her. But I didn't. I was trying to help her. So then I did a stupid thing—"

"You ran away."

His head jerked up. "You knew? You knew about it? How could you know?"

"I didn't know anything. But in such a situation there were only two choices you could make. Either stay or run away. It's obvious you didn't stay."

Doc Linus nodded. "I changed my name, shaved my mustache. All that. Left for the country of the West where hundreds before me had disappeared. Where a man needn't have a past, only the present and the future. But—well, you must know. I know you know. A man can run around the world, maybe even run to the moon, but he can never escape himself."

"That's for sure," Slocum said.

A silence fell while Doc took another pull at his drink.

"I started a whole new life. Nobody here knows about me. Except one person. I don't know how he found out."

"Someone on the council?"

"I am sure he knows."

"Has he said so?"

"No." Doc shook his head. "He doesn't need to. I can tell just by the way he is with me. Little things he drops into a conversation. Like that. I know the son of a bitch knows."

"And that's why you're on the council?"

"It's why I stay on it. I began because I suppose I wanted to do something useful." He got up then and poured himself another drink.

"Take it easy with that stuff," Slocum said.

"Oh, I will. I do. I'm not a bottle puncher."

"So is that why you wanted to see me?"

"I guess so. I wanted to see you actually without really knowing why. The excuse was that the town needs a man like you. But I know I had this other notion behind everything. Someone to talk to, I guess." His sentence died on the last couple of words, and Slocum just barely heard them.

"You want my advice?" Slocum said.

Linus sat down again and looked right at Slocum. He nodded slowly.

"Don't do anything. Stay where you are. See this thing through, whatever it is here with the council and cattle and all, the town. Stay with it. Then, when something is settled, you can see what to do about your life. Meanwhile, don't think any more about what happened. It's done. You did what you thought was the right thing. You tried to help her. It didn't work. Stick with this. If you go back there now, you'll be running away from this here. Do you see that? Get this situation settled; then, if you wish, you can still go back." He paused. "But don't run away again."

"You are saying that if I went back to face the music that I'd be running away again?"

"In the way you'd be doing it, yes. Because something in you wants to run away from here. You mustn't.

It's the running away that's the problem. You can go back home any time and face whatever is there. But you are in the middle of something here, and there are people depending on you. I'm talking about decent people. Your patients and others, not the double-dealers and crooked land promoters and that bunch. Leave here with clean hands, and your hands will be clean when you go back home."

A silence fell into the room now, until presently it was broken by a scratching at the door.

Without a word, Doc got up and walked to the door and opened it.

"Your cat have a name?" Slocum asked.

"Hamlet."

"Interesting name."

"I figure he's a Danish cat."

"How do you figure that?" Slocum asked.

" 'Cause he's got that name."

Slocum looked closely at his companion, realizing that Doc had taken in a good bit of the booze.

"Thanks for listening to me, Slocum. I will take your advice."

"Let it be your own advice," Slocum said firmly. "I don't want credit."

"Good enough then."

"I'll take that drink you offered. And then you can tell me the rest of what's on your mind."

Doc fetched another glass and poured. "I am asking you to be sheriff of Eagle Pass."

"You are asking? What about the council?"

"I am asking."

"But you don't have the power or likely the connections to get me in."

"You can be a deputy. The council in this town has

the power in the absence of a working sheriff to appoint
a deputy, or maybe even more than one. I could look
that up."

"Does the council know you're asking me this?"

Doc shook his head. "Glendenning likely suspects.
But I also know the rest want you. Your name came
up. I mean in that respect, that you've got a reputation
for straight shooting."

"That's why they tried to railroad me into a necktie
party, is it?"

"That's what shows they're a bunch of damn fools.
Except Glendenning. He's not a fool. He's just a son
of a bitch."

Slocum studied it a moment.

"You see," Linus continued. "You have to have an
election for sheriff, whereas a town marshal has to be
appointed by the government. On the other hand, the
town council—here anyway—can appoint deputies in
the absence of a sheriff. As in the present case, with
Mulrooney dead. Then, of course, the deputy can act
as sheriff. Get it?"

"I sure do."

"Will you take the job?"

"Are you meaning to tell me that the same bunch of
buggers that tried to pin the murder of my friend Clyde
Mulrooney on me will now want me to sign on as a
deputy?"

Doc nodded.

"Jesus Christ! Well, I will say they got balls, if no
brains or common sense at all."

Doc ran his hand along the side of his face. "See, I
believe the council members view that episode as an
unfortunate one, and they may even regret it. I believe
they do, though not on your account. Even so, they're

still asking for help. And I am, too, even more so than them."

He paused, gazing into the middle of the room. "It is difficult to know what to do at certain times. As Mr. Shakespeare put it: 'To be or not to be.' Eh?"

"Or are they wanting me to be deputy so's they can keep an eye on me?"

A grin broke out on Linus's worried face. "Slocum, you are a man who I do believe understands human nature a helluva lot better than most of us."

For a moment Slocum regarded the doctor as though he were listening to something inside himself. Then, totally deadpan, he said very simply, "I just do what I am able to do, mostly trying to keep free of 'that disease that is beyond your practice,' Doctor. If I may borrow from your favorite source."

And at that they both had a chuckle.

Finally, they were quiet and they both sat watching Hamlet stretching in the rays of the sun that came through the window of the office and spilled onto the floor.

All that could be heard was the ticking of the clock on Doc Linus's desk.

Slocum could feel the doctor's impatience and concern building.

And finally Linus said, "Will you do it then? Will you agree to become deputy?"

The expression on Slocum's face was neutral as he stood up. "Thanks for the drink," he said. "And the conversation. And—" He looked over at the cat, who was chasing a dustball in the rays of the sun. "In the words of the immortal bard, and you may quote this to your fellow council members, 'I will turn it over.' "

• • •

The self-anointed council, as Doc Linus called them, were meeting in a room at Three-Finger Harold's Fancy Place. "You understand, Linus, I want this man neutralized. I do not want him physically molested. That would surely attract too damn much attention to—well, to us. The council."

"But how, Arthur?" Doc was staring at Arthur Glendenning with an expression of half amazement and a good part loathing, which he was trying to cover up. "He's told me he will think it over. Now, at least that isn't a flat no. It means he hasn't particularly taken sides. Right?"

"And Linus, I think it would help our—uh—enterprise, that is to say, the planning of the council, if you did not go off making decisions on your own. In the future, please be so thoughtful as to let me—us—know what you would like to do, or what you think might be a good plan of action, so that we can all share in it."

The reprimand brought instant color to Doc's neck, cheeks, the roots of his hair. He would have liked to walk over and smash the smart-aleck son of a bitch right in his puffy little mouth.

"I believe I told you the process of my thought, Arthur. The opportunity to talk with Slocum offhand, innocently so to say, suddenly appeared, and I struck while the iron was hot. A coldly planned, premeditated move on our part would have had the opposite effect. This way he is not a complete ally, but he is not against us. That is definite, and that is why I acted as I did, and it is also why I would do it again should the need arise!"

He had not intended to blow off such a head of steam, but his words simply pumped up his justification to the point where he felt he'd had no alternative than to speak to Slocum the way he had. But of course Sophe Linus knew he was speaking from emotion and not cool sense. He didn't care. He was thoroughly fed up, with Glendenning especially, but also with the other pissants.

A silence fell over the group of five. Glendenning knew very well how to take advantage; indeed, he had a genius for using silence as a weapon. He leaned back in his chair now, lips pursed, lightly, almost soundlessly whistling a ditty, examining his fingernails, placing his long forefinger along the side of his nose and now holding his slate-gray eyes directly on Dr. Sophocles Linus.

"Thank you, Sophocles," he said with the emotion and deadly accuracy of an asp.

Then, suddenly placing a big smile on his face, he stood up and walked over to Doc, grabbed his arm with one hand, and shook hands with his other. It was a vigorous handshake, as he pumped Doc's arm up and down, slapped him jovially on the shoulder, and beamed at him. "Let's bury it, my friend! This is no time for fighting among ourselves. Frankly, I think you did absolutely the right thing! You disarmed Slocum. You've shown the way to the rest of us! And you have shown Slocum that the Eagle Pass Council is something to be reckoned with."

Doc's surprise at the switch in Glendenning's behavior almost did him in. He recovered, however, and smiled back, feeling his "good humor" as though it had literally been painted on his face; he even mumbled a word or two. But Glendenning had so skillfully reversed the field that Doc wasn't sure whether he was ahead or behind. And he realized painfully that the man really knew how to handle a hot situation. For in a few words and gestures, and in less than ten minutes of time, he had put the entire council right back into his pocket.

"Well, let's order some more drinks then," Glendenning was saying, "and get down to business. Has everybody had enough to eat?"

A round of jovial agreement followed; yes, everyone was fed. And it was time for something to warm the veins, the cockles of the soul.

They were in a private room at Three-Finger Harold's place. And they had already commented on the good quality of the food, the service, and the booze.

As they were enjoying more than one or even two superior kinds of imported brandy, the meeting loosened considerably, and even Doc Linus felt better.

Glendenning held high his glass. "To us! There are few like us; and for all we know, maybe few like us!" And he chortled, while his companions laughed roundly, and all drank.

"Homer, would you see that the door is locked?"

Homer Content rose swiftly, kicked his foot against a chair leg, but recovered and walked to the door and locked it.

"We will not be disturbed now," Glendenning said, as he leaned forward, placing his forearms on the table and letting his eyes take in each of the company.

"Gentlemen, let us just review some of the activity that's been going on. The Morgan Dyce herd is just outside town as you all know. But I have news that Cole Berringer has paid him a visit. I can't for the life of me figure why Berringer, who I've been told is an ancient enemy of Dyce's, would be visiting that gentleman. Unless the two of them have buried the hatchet in some way."

"Those boys will bury the hatchet in each other or if they're together, they'll bury it in somebody else. I wouldn't trust either one of 'em," said Homer Content, "far as I could throw that little pinto pony that just foaled out at Sam Rogers's place."

"You all know Berringer and how he feels about the town and the council, and you also know how he feels about Eagle Pass becoming a shipping point," Glendenning said. "We best keep a eye on that man."

He paused, again running his index finger along the side of his nose.

"Thing is," Ludlow Franks said, "thing is, what the hell is them two hawks doing together? Does Berringer think he's going to talk Dyce out of shipping through Eagle Pass? Hell, we got the railway coming right in. They ain't a thing can stop that Double Back D outfit from shipping."

"Maybe there isn't. And I do believe you're right," Glendenning said. "But there could be one thing would stop it."

"You mean—?" Doc suddenly raised his eyebrows as the frightful thought struck him.

"I do mean a stampede. All that man has to do is stampede that herd of his through town, and we're wiped out."

"Jesus!"

"But he'll run the hell out of those beeves. They won't be worth shipping to hell after a stampede like that!"

"There is, of course, the possibility of calling the army." Glendenning's statement fell into the group like a thunderclap.

Homer Content's jaw sprang open like a barn door. Calvin Phobis looked blindly into the cloud of thick smoke that he had just blown after drawing on his luxuriant panatela. Ludlow Franks blinked rapidly as though to forestall the picture that wanted to come into his mind. Doc Linus, who had been daydreaming about the pleasures of Consuelo's delicious body, was suddenly jerked back into the room and the grim possibility that Arthur Glendenning had raised.

"The army!" Doc almost breathed the words. "God, what a thought!" He stared at Glendenning. "The army, eh." His tone calmer now. "You mean, martial law established. The election run under the surveillance of the military. And like all that, eh?"

"It's a possibility." Glendenning's tone was easy, almost oily. "You know, we wanted a strong man as sheriff when we heard the Double Back D was coming. Those cowboys when they hit a town—well, you know how that is. I know some of you have even been there."

"I been in Ellsworth," Phobis said. And his perennial white Stetson wagged from side to side. "It ain't no country dance time. It is hell, boys. Hell!"

"I seen Dodge and Abilene," put in Ludlow Franks. "Like a herd of wild buffalo stampeded through it by the time the boys got done treeing the town."

Doc had seen it, but said nothing. His grin was like acid on his face as he began to see more of Glendenning's plan.

"Doc, you were in Cimarron, I've heard," Glendenning said.

"What's your plan, Arthur? We all know what happens when a town gets a passel of starving trail hands busting in. What are you suggesting we do about it?"

And he felt the firmness in his own words, in the quality of his voice. It was getting down to the nub now and he felt he was ready to call Glendenning's hand.

He was watching Glendenning's Adam's apple and saw it pump. "We probably have got at best forty-eight hours to get ready."

"We've had a helluva lot more time than that to get ready," Doc said, leaning forward on the table. "But we've been slopping around with this Slocum business, and Mulrooney. No, just a minute!" He was holding up his hand to stop Phobis, who had started to speak. "The trouble is we've been shilly-shallying over whether we want Slocum to take over. The trouble being—" And he raised his voice this time to top Franks, who wanted to say something. "The trouble has been that we're afraid we'll have a grizzly by the tail. And gents, I do believe we will. Slocum is no sweetheart who'll play tiddlywinks with us boys, but he will bring order, if any man can. I'm for it. I'm for getting him. Offer him anything."

He was watching Glendenning as he spoke, seeing the smile that, while remaining on the man's face, went cold, as though the life in it had been exchanged for ice.

"Are you saying you want a man for sheriff here who might quite possibly have murdered the former holder of that office?" Glendenning's words fell onto the table like chips bumping a big raise in the game.

"I am saying that."

"I dunno," Cal Phobis said, again wagging his white hat.

Homer Content said, "He would have to report to us. It would be dead wrong to give such a man a free hand."

"But—!" Ludlow Franks was holding out his palms as though trying to reason by pointing out the impossible lying right before them. "But will he agree? And will we be able to keep him bridled? And what about the army? Eh? And, there's something else I want to bring up, and which—"

But Glendenning now boldly cut him off. "I'll take over that, Ludlow, inasmuch as I have new information." He paused, a rather cold grin on his face as he tightened his lips and his shaven chin puckered.

This is it, Sophe Linus thought. He'd been waiting for it. The element that made the mare go, by God. He wanted more than he'd ever wanted anything to interrupt, to cut Glendenning off, to get the word in first, for he realized that while most of them probably suspected something, only he had any hard evidence on it.

But he was too late. Glendenning said, "Let us not forget the matter of—uh—the activities of the gentleman we know as Tyrone Tyrone and his enterprise, which he engages in fortnightly, and sometimes monthly at Snake River Creek. If we call in the United States Army, might we very well not be opening a box of goods that we would rather leave closed?"

The silence that fell upon the group of five was like a fog. That, at any rate, was how Doc Linus felt it. One's thoughts moved, but in slow motion, and with an effort. It was as though he didn't want to think. He could see that the others were experiencing something similar. They sat in their chairs like stones at a funeral, simply being there as part of the terrain. He tried to think of Consuelo, but found even that difficult.

Finally, more to break the deadly moment than for any other reason, he pushed back his chair and stood up. "Be back, boys." And he left the room to relieve himself.

The air outside on the way to the outhouse was warm but clean. It was on his way back that he saw the big man entering the back door of Two-Ton Priscilla's Premier Saloon Drinking and Eating Emporium.

Suddenly he knew that John Slocum must be the man in charge. Suddenly he realized with absolute clarity the game Glendenning was playing. Glendenning—and it was as obvious now as the weather in a tornado— was running his own private game. Sophocles Linus realized with every fiber of himself that he had known this all along, but he had only felt it, not realized it with his intellect, had not yet been able to express it in words. But now it was as clear as a mountain spring. Mention of Tyrone Tyrone had simply triggered it in his thought, shot what was vague into a picture as clear as the sky he was looking at overhead. His thoughts raced. He had known and yet not known all along that Glendenning was working only for himself.

The son of a bitch! And Sophe Linus had a smile on his face as he walked back into Three-Finger Harold's Fancy Place.

The silence remained in the back room when he entered. The drinks, Doc noticed, had been well addressed during his absence, and there was a smile behind the quiet expression on Glendenning's thin face.

"Saw somebody slipping into Two-Ton Priscilla's place," he said as he sat down.

He waited a moment to let it hit them, and then he said, "Looks to me like we'd better move on Mr. John Slocum, I mean like maybe perhaps right now."

6

Slocum had seen Sophe Linus just before he had been seen himself, and he had made no effort to hide from Doc's view. At the same time, he had felt no need to acknowledge the other's presence. The code always allowed privacy and noninterference to take precedence over social recognition. It was a sensitivity that Slocum appreciated, and cultivated in himself, but which he also saw was slackening in the world in which he moved. The world of the frontier was not as it used to be. The changes were slight, but they were definite. It made him wonder. Why? The buffalo were gone, and so were the beaver; and soon the Indian would follow. Certainly the frontiersman had almost as good as disappeared. And the land, he thought. The land would go, too. The railroads would take over from the trappers and buffalo killers. And the land grabbers and promoters and the politicians would complete the "civilizing" which was always being promoted in the name of that value which, by its very presence, was killing everything in sight. Civilizing the Indian meant something even worse than killing him.

But that was the way it was. He felt not the least sentimentality about it. Indeed, he knew full well that sentimentality was one of the worst elements in the ruin of the land. But these were thoughts he kept to himself. Obviously what was going on was what was wanted.

Meanwhile, there was the situation at Eagle Pass, and he had been called to an audience with the massive Two-Ton Priscilla Handles.

She was in one of the back rooms of her establishment. He found her sitting at the round, baize-topped table playing solitaire.

As he entered, she didn't look up, but was holding her cards, studying what move to make, and spoke over her shoulder.

"Set."

He seated himself while she continued to look for her play and finally found it. She dropped the card into its place with a grunt, as though releasing some uncomfortable weight.

Then, her large hand almost covering the cards she was holding, she placed the deck carefully at her side. Her eyes lifted. And the two of them sat there, across the round table from each other, not saying a word.

Finally, the lady spoke. "Well, what kin I do fer you, mister?"

"You can tell me why you sent me a message to come see you," Slocum said coolly.

"Huh!"

Another silence fell, and then he pushed back his chair and started to get to his feet.

"What's yer hurry, mister?"

"I believe in playing my cards, not staring the spots off them," Slocum said. He sat there with his chair pushed back and his hands on his knees, ready to rise.

"Wanted to have a little talk with you," Two-Ton said.

"I'm listening."

Her face moved then, and he figured she was grinning, though he wasn't sure.

"I hear the boys are aimin' for you to be our next lawman."

"Oh?"

"I'm wondering how you might be feelin' about that."

Slocum decided to not play games, so he said, "Told the messenger I'd turn it over."

"And—?" She looked directly at him then, her enormous arms lying like great rolls of dough on the baize-topped table. One or two of her numerous rings glinted from the light coming through the window.

"I am turning it over."

"You're a man what takes his time."

"Things generally go better that way."

"I do believe that is so." She sniffed, her wide nostrils flaring somewhat. Slocum found himself wondering if she was as heavy as Heavy Ham Hamilton, the mule skinner he'd known out in Oro City. Heavy was enormous, maybe bigger than Two-Ton, but more muscle than fat. No man to cross. But a bullet had finished him just as easily as if he'd been a skinny hundred-pounder. Funny, Slocum mused, the thoughts that come into your head in moments such as this.

"I do not believe in wasting my time, Priscilla, though I do favor your company. Still, I got a lot to do. Besides, I hear there'll be some cattle coming through town any day now, and I want to see where I'm going to be."

"That is just what I'm talking about, mister. Where are you going to be? Are you with the cattle shippers, are you with the railroad, or are you with the local ranchers, the town, law, and whatever-they-call-it?"

"Order," Slocum said.

"You are not deaf, dumb, or blind. I know you see what's going on here."

"Do I?"

"You better. It is exactly what you don't see on the surface. Like law and order? Don't be funny. This town is gonna be ripped wide open, and the boys are gonna take over."

"Who do you mean by 'the boys'?" he asked innocently.

"It ain't your sweet little old ladies who go to church and all that. It ain't even some of the merchants in town, men like Tom Corbett, or Frank Forbin, and them. You know who I'm talking about, Slocum."

"I do. But why does that bother you? Do you think they'll shut down your outfit here?"

"I ain't worried about that."

"So—?"

"Fact, I ain't worried about anything. But on the other hand, I am concerned about what those assholes will do once they get legally in office."

"What will they do?"

"You've been around, my friend, so why do I have to explain it to you? You know what happened down in Tombstone, and other places when what they call the law-and-order bunch took over. They started laying on taxes and paybacks from every damn card you dealt, every drink of whiskey, every gal that threw her talent at a customer. You know what I mean. I don't mind paying some protection, but this gang that wants to take over here—and I know damn well you know who I mean—they are greedy. Glendenning—just in case you didn't know—ran Julesburg into the ground, then left. And course, somebody else got the blame for what he done. He got off scot-free. And, my lad, Eagle Pass is ripe for the fucking!" And she added, "Yes, I said 'fucking'!"

"Then you are concerned about your business."

"I'd be a goddamn fool if I wasn't." She sniffed, her shoulders heaving with the effort this time. "There be others 'sides myself who are concerned. I don't give a shit for them, I am talking about yours truly. And I am not above or beneath looking for, askin' for help when needed. You understand now in plain, simple, clear, polite English what the fuck I am sayin' to you!"

"I do." Slocum couldn't restrain his grin as he listened to her, watching her face turn shades from a powdery white to red as her anxiety and anger took over completely.

"Good enough!" She reached for the bottle and poured herself a drink. "There is a glass there," she said, pushing the bottle in his direction.

"What are you asking me to do?" he said. "Not that I'm agreeing to anything; only asking."

"I know. I know. You don't have to get a hard-on, God dammit. I am just sayin' that me, we, this town needs help."

Suddenly, like the passing of a storm, she was silent, she was still. She sat there looking down at her hands lying on the table, while he poured himself a drink. Her entire mass echoed a silence he had not imagined she possessed. Incredibly, there was something almost religious in the way she was sitting, in the way she was looking down at her hands, and he asked himself what it was. Her posture? The bend of her head, her lowered shoulders, which he had always seen held so high and defensive yet offensive at the same time? Or was it just atmosphere? He in no way felt sentimental about her, not sorry or pitying or anything like that.

"I don't want you to do anything, Slocum," she said quietly then. "I guess I'm just sayin' it'd be nice if you didn't do anything. I mean with those sons of bitches."

"Glendenning."

"Him and the ones he's working with. Not the bunch here. I'm talking about the men back East, the railroad men. The ones who get the immigrants coming, promising them the moon and giving them lies. Don't get me wrong. I am not concerned about humanity. I don't give a damn for people, except what I can get out of them. But people like Glendenning and his crowd, the land grabbers, the speculators, the money promoters— I am talking about the bastards who sell you money, and meaning by that they sell people and buy them— I don't want them doing that around here."

"Are your games straight?" Slocum asked.

She looked up at him then. "Slocum, you know just as well as I do that if a successful gambling house kept all its games straight just where in hell would the excitement of beating it come from?"

To his astonishment, he found a note for him at the desk when he returned to the Longhorn Cottage. It was, of course, not the fact of receiving a note that furnished his great surprise, but the signature. He felt something thumping in his chest as he read her name. And it said she would be waiting for him—if he was free—in the dining room.

She was sitting at the far end of the room, with her profile to the entrance, and he got a good look at her fine features before she saw him.

"What a nice surprise!" he said, taking her hand and looking down into those deep brown eyes which were like wells. But then, as he sat down facing her, his thoughts began to arrange themselves under the possibility of her dangerous ride into town, and what she was doing here.

"It's none of my business, young lady, but you could have been running a big risk riding into town all by yourself."

"I know." She smiled at him, like a child caught at mischief. "Stash insisted on coming along, but I told him no. And Uncle Pete, also. But you see, I did have to come in to get some medicine for Uncle Pete. With all the excitement going on, we forgot to get it, and he's about to run out. I figured if I get it back to him tomorrow it'll do him."

He could feel the wave of warmth coming from her and he wanted to do nothing more than just be with her. Thus they sat in silence while simply looking at each other, and waiting for the waitress to come over.

Finally she did, and Slocum ordered a cup of coffee.

"I've had two already," Ali said when he asked. "This is my second, that is."

Another silence fell on them, and it was nice, he thought, simply to be with her.

"It's nice to be here," she said. "I didn't know when, or even if I'd be seeing you again."

"But I thought we'd decided that I was going to help out. Remember? Or have you changed your mind?"

"Oh no. Not at all." And her cheeks reddened just a little. "It's just I didn't want you to feel beholden."

"I don't, Miss Mulrooney."

"That's very nice, Mr. Slocum."

"I didn't ask you if you'd like something to eat."

"I don't, really. And anyway, it's not suppertime yet." She had been leaning forward a little on the other side of the table, with her hands in her lap, and now she sat up. "I'm sorry. I've been thoughtless."

He looked surprised. "How so?"

"I know you must have a lot to do, you must be very busy, and here I am taking up your time. I'm sorry. Forgive me. Please, I have engaged a room here, and so I can go there, and besides, I might take a walk. I've got plenty to do."

"Where's your room? I mean, is it a good one? I've heard that some of the rooms are more like closets." And he looked down at their empty coffee cups.

"Well, the reason I've come in here is because I had to wait while they made the room up. Someone had vacated, and it wasn't quite ready when I first came in."

"Oh. I see. Well, let me walk you to your door," he said gallantly. "I'll walk you home."

They both chuckled at that. "Have you luggage, miss?"

"It's only a few things in my sack."

He had taken her sack and stood aside to let her go out of the dining room first.

"You don't have to carry that," she said.

"It's terribly heavy," he said, tossing it up and then catching it one-handed, "but I'll manage. Let's get your room key."

She didn't say anything when he escorted her up the stairs, carrying her small sack of overnight things. And when they got to her room, he took the key from her hand and unlocked and opened the door.

"I'll just check your window to see that you're in a good place."

"How do you mean?" she asked.

And when he turned to answer her, he saw the sunlight streaming into the room, catching her hair, and lighting her as though she was standing in the middle of everything.

"You're beautiful," he said.

He saw her breath catch. "Is—is that why you're checking the window?" she asked.

They both had a laugh at that.

"I'm checking it to see that no one can climb up here. I don't mean to frighten you, but the town is getting ready for the cattle drive, and you never know how these things can go."

"Thank you. I understand."

He had returned from the window and was now standing in front of her.

"I didn't tell you just right about you're being beautiful," he said.

"You mean, you're taking it back! Well, I don't think that's very nice." And she made a face.

"I mean to correct what I said," he insisted. "You're not beautiful. You are very beautiful!"

"Oh—" And as he stepped toward her, she dropped her eyes to his mouth and followed his lips as he took her in his arms.

The kiss was long as they melted together. And their lips clung.

"I want to lock the door," she whispered against his chest.

"Let's both lock it."

And with their arms around each other they walked to the door and turned the key.

"Leave it in the lock," he said as she started to take it out.

"Oh?"

"Someone might have another key, a cleaning lady or somebody, and might think the room is unoccupied."

As he led her to the bed, she said, "In a situation such as this one, Mr. Slocum, I feel it's very fortunate to be with someone who has a good bit of experience in such matters."

"And I—I feel it's a good thing to be with the best person and the most beautiful that you could find in the whole of the west, or east, or north, or south."

And their lips closed together as his hands reached down and began unbuttoning her shirt.

In moments they were naked, except for her underwear, and she had started to take that off herself as he pulled down the covers of the bed.

The next thing she had taken his hard member in her hand and was leading him by it as she lay down with her legs apart and guided him inside her.

Her giving was total, as was his. Gently, he stroked her with his rigid erection, and with his entire body, feeling, and even thought behind those simple, delicious movements. She was tight and moist at the same time, so he had no trouble entering and reaching all the way.

"Oh, thank you, thank you," she whispered into his mouth before he closed it with his kissing. His tongue reached deep into her throat. "Oh John—" As she gasped for air, hugging him with her arms and legs as her buttocks undulated and bounced off the bed, while the springs creaked and complained at the exercise.

But neither of them were bothered by the noise, if indeed they even heard it. For now they were stroking faster, though not racing. He rode her gently, firmly, and each time to the hilt. But also now drawing his great member almost all the way out of her squeezing vagina, just to the edge of the head of his organ, so that twice she begged him not to "go away." And of course, he had no intention of leaving her.

Now he moved a little more quickly, their come lubricating their movement with utter delight as he pounded his balls against her buttocks each time he drove down and up and deep. She wiggled and stroked right with him in absolute delight, as her little cries of impossible ecstasy told him. Until they were forced by the power and momentum of their exploding passion to stroke faster, deeper, higher, harder, and softer at the same time—it was difficult to tell which, and it didn't matter, for all that mattered was that they were coming and coming and coming—until every last drop had been squirted from his pounding organ and from her begging, soaking, thrashing buttocks and cunt.

In delicious ecstasy and satiation they lay totally immobile, unable even to lift a finger.

They lay there still locked in embrace, still gently kissing each other on the eyes, the ears, the lips. Her fingers touched his lips as she settled herself farther down in the bed, her arms and legs still embracing him, while his hands were holding her head, covering her ears, though not so she couldn't hear, but as a caress. Now his fingers played with her delightful earlobes, the hair at the nape of her neck, and his tongue licked the corners of her half open lips, until she grabbed it with her lips and sucked.

They rested.

"May I lie on top of you?"

"Am I heavy?"

"Oh, no. I just thought it would be nice."

"I think it would be great," he said, coming up on his hands and knees, and then turning onto his back.

The next thing he knew she was between his legs with her fist around his instantly rising penis, and now with her lips circling its head while her tongue licked out into the little slit at the very apex of its length.

"If you keep doing that, he'll come in your mouth."

"I want him to. I want to suck him and eat him and drink him. Oh, my God, my God!"

And she was down on him, taking him all the way in her mouth, into the deepest part of her throat, as far as he could go. And sucking all the way out to its tip and then, outside, licking down his long, rigid shaft, then back up and down again with his joystick this time inside her mouth and throat, sucking its full length. While his finger explored the inside of her soaking vagina, feeling, stroking, wiggling it while her buttocks bounced with joy.

Then, somehow without either of them knowing how it happened, she was up on her hands and knees and he was mounting her from the rear, driving all the way in and up and she was practically standing on her head and he was pumping his thick club all the way. And now with its head all the way in and up as far as it would go, while he wiggled it back and forth and she gasped and squirmed and finally cried out in her unbearable delight as he probed and fucked her till she was on the point of begging for mercy, and finally did. "Give it, it, come, come, comecomecome—oh God, commmmmme—"

And they did.

And lay side by side, soaking wet, with come all over their bellies and buttocks and crotches, and the delicious smell of it in their nostrils.

"Love," she whispered. "My love—"

7

In the predawn, Morgan Dyce was already up watching the wrangler bringing in the remuda for the men who'd be working the herd. He was standing swing-hipped by his saddle rigging, which was lying on the ground, when E. T. Crimmins, his trail boss, came up.

"Heered you ordered the men to get the herd movin'," E. T. said.

"We'll be going in today," the boss of the Double Back D brand said.

"Well, good enough. The men are gettin' real raspy."

"So I notice."

"We got clearance and we'll head right for the pens?"

"I mean you an' me and a couple of the boys will be goin' into town. Otis can handle the herd and the men here."

"Hunh—" E. T.'s eyebrows lifted some at that and his mouth pursed. "The cattle is gettin' just as onnery as the men," he said.

"We'll be ridin' time I get my dun saddled. Bring them two with you. I want them to see the layout."

The ramrod of the Double Back D squinted at his boss then. "You sure? Mebbe somebody in town might know them."

"Crimmins, get your ass movin' and don't hand me no argument on it!"

E. T. knew better than to say another word, and in a moment or two he sent orders to Honniger and Deltus, the two hard cases the boss had picked down in the Indian Territory.

Ten minutes later, give or take, the four were riding out.

Otis, who stayed behind to run things, spat thoughtfully after them. "Boys, I do believe we are in for a duster." Otis spoke those words to no one in particular, yet with a heavy feeling in his guts, a feeling of big trouble coming up. It had been building ever since they'd reached Crazy Wolf Crossing. Without thinking anything more about it, Otis, an old hand and a good one, checked his six-gun and the Henry in his rifle scabbard hanging on his saddle.

Meanwhile, the four men were raising dust on their way into town.

Morgan Dyce, in the lead, knew that the Lazy CB outrider had spotted their departure. Cole Berringer wasn't taking any chances, and he'd had outriders watching the Double Back D herd ever since they'd reached Crazy Wolf Crossing.

It was about halfway through the forenoon when they walked their horses up the long draw and into the protection of a stand of pine and fir that looked down on Eagle Pass at the end of the long basin.

"We'll split here. You two come in this afternoon from the other side of the butte. Yonder." Morgan Dyce pointed.

"But they seen us all together," E. T. pointed out. "That the way you want it?"

"If I didn't, I wouldn't of done it," snapped his boss. Then, "I want them wonderin'. I don't want them too sure. I for sure don't want them sure about anything."

"You're saying you don't want Berringer to be sure you're gonna play it his way?"

"He never was sure. He's no dumbbell. He never was sure. But I lullabied him for a bit. See. Now he's no longer so suspicious on account of him hearin' we're riding in with these here two, and splitting up—see— he'll figger that's my play."

"Don't get it, but never mind," E. T. said.

"What don't you git?"

"He'll see you ain't gonna do what you said you were going to."

"That is what I want him to see. He is relaxed with it now, which he wouldn't be if he thought I'd gone along with him. See, now he figgers I'll cross him, and he'll be looking for that."

"But how will that surprise him?" E. T. Crimmins was regretting that he'd ever raised the subject, but he was stuck with it now.

"For Christ sake, it will surprise him out of his goddamn britches for me to be doin' what the son of a bitch wanted me to do in the first place. He knows I agreed too easy, so he expects me to cross him. Get it, do you! And it's that that'll ream it to him right up the ass, by God! I have got to figurin' I might just take an' bust that goddamn town wide open!"

And the boss of the Double Back D kicked his tough little dun into an easy canter, spitting downwind as he did so. He was feeling pleased that he'd picked the dun this morning; he was a fine little cutting horse Morgan Dyce had broken himself.

In the big log ranch house at the Lazy CB located just north and east of Whistle Creek, Cole Berringer, tall, tough, and lean as a whip, stood looking out of the window at the big country spread before him. It was a big window for a big country, as he was fond of saying. But Cole appreciated the window for other reasons, the main being that he could watch a good portion of the approaches to the Lazy CB, another that he could see the corrals where the men would be working fresh horseflesh.

Behind him, almost across the big room, his cattle foreman Tyson Wills stood waiting for orders.

Ty Wills was used to waiting. He was a ramrod from the old school and he'd been with Cole Berringer a good quarter century. They'd opened the land around Eagle Pass and Whistle Creek. The first whites, they'd fought the Arapaho, the Cheyenne, and sometimes even the Sioux. Ty Wills remembered all the trouble with Morgan Dyce, as well.

"What you make of the new men?" Berringer suddenly asked, still looking out the window. "Damn! That tall one don't know the ass of that hoss from its head. Jesus!"

And he turned back into the room to face his ramrod. "Assholes. Well, we'll ditch 'em soon as this here business is done with."

"You sure you want to keep them, Cole?" Ty Wills had been wanting to ask that question for a good long while, and now he'd finally said it.

The boss of the Lazy CB had taken out his makings and was building himself a smoke. Done with it, he tossed the little sack of tobacco to his foreman and then handed him the papers.

"You can bet your sweet ass that Dyce has hired himself extra help."

"That's for sure." Ty Wills had built his cigarette, suddenly remembering his old man, who'd had one arm but still built his own smokes, laying it all out on his thigh and working with one hand. And he was real fast, too.

"Jeff Hanks seen one of them new hands, gunhands what Dyce hired. Feller could just about handle his hoss; a big sorrel what looked like he was ready for crow bait. Still, Jeff said the man wasn't riding him too easy."

"But we ain't concerned with how he handles hosses," Berringer pointed out, "but how he handles those two guns." He cleared his throat, hawking, and then spat a big gob of phlegm into the nearby cuspidor. "And also whether or not he's got more'n them two."

"You thinking of getting ourselves more'n a pair, are you?"

"Two is enough. You get more than two, you've got a army, and people will cause trouble. I mean like in town."

"Got'cha."

"Question is whether Dyce is crazy enough to stampede his cattle through the town and take over with his wild cowboys. I do bet more than a few of them crazy Texas boys know one end of a six-gun from the other."

"Still, he hired a couple gunmen, and maybe more, for all we know," Ty said.

"Maybe to keep attention off his regular hands," said Cole. "Hell, I dunno."

He hawked and spat again.

"I still dunno what the hell he's doin' way up north here. There is other shipping points, and we ain't even started yet. What you reckon he's got in mind?"

Ty Wills had known Cole Berringer a long time, and they'd been through just about all a man could go through together, but still he didn't like saying it. But he did.

"Maybe looks like it might be he is after you," he said.

"Might. But there ain't no might or maybe I am after his ass!"

A silence fell into the room then, while Cole Berringer stood looking out the big window. His ranch foreman stood behind him. Ty Wills had finished his smoke, had stubbed it out between his calloused thumb and forefinger, and now stood looking at his boss's back.

"You figger yet what Dyce's play is?" the man at the window said.

"All I know is he wants to ship, and that could be in a day or two, course dependin' when the train gets in. But he can bring his herd in any time now and keep 'em in the yards."

"I dunno when the cattle cars are due," Cole Berringer said, turning from the window and facing his foreman. "Cattle can't stay there too long. But the latest I heard was tomorrow, for the train. Any case, I reckon you can bet yer ass Dyce is workin' with that son of a bitch Glendenning."

"I heerd their election is scheduled for tomorrow," Ty said.

"I heard that. I also heard they got no one to run for sheriff except a couple volunteers who don't know one end of a six-gun from th' other."

"There is talk of that feller Slocum."

"Hunh."

Cole Berringer had turned his back to the room again and was staring out the big window. He spoke now to his foreman without turning around, without much expression in his voice. Just words. Each one, or even several together, not amounting to much—at least so thought Ty Wills—yet the whole adding up to something much more than its parts. The whole hitting him right in his guts.

"Tell what you would do," Cole Berringer said, facing the long green-and-brown vista beyond the big window. "How you figure Dyce'll play it? And what the hell is that council bunch up to? I have heerd they, or one of 'em, I dunno which, took a ride out to Belly Creek to have a powwow with Rising Horse." He belched suddenly. "How d'you read all that? And this feller Slocum. You figger he might be a Association man? Maybe a marshal from Fort Tenny?"

From behind him, Ty Wills saw him reach to his shirt pocket for his makings.

"There is gonna be blood spilling in town," the rancher continued. "Not that it's anything new. But there is so damn many things going. Like the Quarter Circle M an' Pete Mulrooney. He ain't about to 'llow that outfit out of his hands. But you know that range is what I have had my eye on this good while."

"We need it," Ty said, glad to be getting a supportive word into the long monologue. "I know you bin wanting that range. But I know same as you that hell'll freeze over and melt again and still freeze up 'fore Mulrooney'll let loose of it, no matter what you offer."

"Tell me what you see, Ty. I got a real funny feeling

about that Glendenning feller. I have heard he was trying to work out some land deal with the 'rapahoes. With Rising Horse. And I know he made a offer to Clyde Mulrooney, and he's tried making a offer for this here."

"That's what I know," Ty said, his face grim.

"What I am wonderin' about is why the delay. Things are moving much too slow." He turned around to face the room.

"Seems to me everything's going too damn fast," said Ty Wills.

"Wrong. Those cattle could of been brought right into that graze around the south side of town. And when I rode out there and seen Dyce I seen by his layout they was waitin' on something. Course, I didn't let on. But I handled him like I didn't notice. Spoke to him about riding his cowboys in and treeing the town. Something like that."

"Jesus," said Ty Wills. "He could take you up on that."

"He won't."

"How come?"

"I can see he's got other plans."

"Do you know what?"

"Wish I did. The only thing I can think of is he's tied in somehow with that bunch that's trying to take over running Eagle Pass. Course this feller Slocum coming in and bringing all that trouble about Clyde Mulrooney could of screwed their plan, least for the while."

"You're saying that Dyce might be working with the council bunch."

"Why else did he pick Eagle Pass to ship when he's always gone to Caldwell and Darren? Leastways, that's how come I sent him the message that I wanted to meet with him. I wanted him to know damn sure he wasn't getting away with anything."

"You're sayin' Dyce could be up to somethin' with the council people in Eagle Pass."

"Council? Mebbe. Glendenning? I wouldn't trust that man far as I can spit in a windstorm." He was silent. Then suddenly without any warning, he erupted. "God dammit to hell!" He spun around to face his foreman, his mouth working. "Goddamn those fuckers! They have come in here and grabbed up land and taken over the towns and fucked up everybody all over the place from here to breakfast! Goddamn them! Goddamn them!"

"Who? Who you talkin' about?"

"The railroad, the land grabbers and land speculators, the railtown builders with their goddamn shacks comin' in everywhere on their flatcars and throwin' up towns and gettin' one town set against the other. Each one wantin' to be county seat like, and bringing in all them people promising them the world. Free land! You ever read one of them papers they hand out to all the people comin' in from Europe? Promise them heaven in a dust bowl. You hear it everywhere. Thick topsoil that'll grow mountains of corn and spuds and God knows what else! Exceptin' what they got when they git here? Topsoil thinner than a wet gunnysack. That's what they got. Nothin'! But them speculators and land operators and dealers, they bin and they still be doin' it—sellin' fire to the Devil hisself. With by God a free pitchfork thrown in for any amount over a thousand— or whatever!"

Only once before in all the years he'd known Cole Berringer had his foreman seen him that angry; only that time when his daughter had taken up with that ne'er-do-well saddlebum and got herself knocked up. The old man was ready to kill; and would have, if that sly bugger hadn't skedaddled. Cole Berringer was ready then to take on the whole world. And now, he was pretty close to the same.

Ty had heard it before. All of it. Over and over. And he knew the truth of it, too, and felt the same, though without getting so burned up over it. The old man really was ready to charge hell with his bare hands; meaning the speculators, the promoters, the snake oil salesmen, the fast talking dudes and the sharpie dice switchers and card markers. But especially those bastard land riggers who gulled the immigrants, even sending their agents overseas to get them in their homeland and talk them into coming to America to populate the frontier and get their life savings funneled right into those hungry, greedy pockets of the sharps. Ty knew that it wasn't so much that Cole Berringer cared a damn about the poor and the immigrants looking for new homes as he did for his own acres, which he was using without paying a cent, it being government land.

Still, Ty Wills knew the story forward and backward, having heard it so many times from his boss. Even so, he sided with the cattlemen. For they were here first. Ty Wills had also fought the Arapaho and the Cheyenne and the Sioux. He, too, had been there when there was still virgin land. The government, the men in Washington and other places didn't know a damn thing about the frontier; they were crooks, anyway, and always siding with the big cattle combines run by men in New York and Philadelphia and even as far away as London in England.

In a calmer tone now, Berringer resumed. "It is easy to see Glendenning is counting big money in back of him. I mean, money that don't know a cow from a hoss, but knows the price, by God. The sons of bitches always knows the price!" He hawked, clearing his throat, and spat vigorously into the spittoon that stood waiting near his big feet. "That son of a bitch, trying to buy me out that time."

"He try again since then?" Ty Wills asked.

"Yup. An' more than once!"

There came a knock at the door. And when Ty Wills walked over and opened it, he found Joe Goshen, the horse wrangler standing with his hat in his hand.

"Rider coming in. Tod tolt me to tell Mr. Berringer."

"Anybody know who it is?"

But before the wrangler could answer, the front door of the house opened down the hallway and another rider appeared; it was the outrider from along the northern fence line.

"That feller Slocum is coming in," he said. "Couple of the boys tried to stop him riding into the beeves we got bunched up on the northern line, and he busted 'em. Said he was lookin' for Mulrooney stock, and if he found any, he was gonna take it, like right now."

"Where is he now?" Cole Berringer's deep voice broke through the open door and Ty Wills stepped aside.

"He oughtta be here any time now. Said he was riding in to see you, Mr. Berringer."

"Good enough then. Let him in when he comes."

They stood looking at each other as the door closed.

"I understand you want to inspect my stock. That right?" The words emerged cold and hard from Cole Berringer as he stood like a tree in the middle of his office.

"That is what I've been doing," Slocum said. "On behalf of Pete Mulrooney and his Quarter Circle M brand."

"You know you're trespassing."

"So are those couple dozen beeves with their Quarter Circle M brand changed to Lazy CB."

"Can you prove that, mister?"

"I don't need to, Berringer, and I am sure not going to waste my time with that nonsense. You know same as I do what I'm saying to you. Also, there is more than likely more. You know that, too. So let's cut the cackle, and get down to it."

"Down to what, mister?"

He saw that Berringer was taking it about as he had expected. But there was no other way, and he had decided on a frontal attack. Sitting down talk never got a man anywhere in this kind of situation. A man like Cole Berringer understood only one thing. A force. A force greater, tougher, swifter than his own. Slocum had hit him right between the eyes.

"An' what you figurin' to do about that, young feller?"

Slocum immediately caught the sneering laughter in the cattleman's words.

"You got any authority to ride in here and tell me this kind of bullshit?"

"I am foreman of the Mulrooney spread, first. That is my authority. And second, I am here and I am telling you. That iron work wouldn't fool a blind man."

"So what you figure you're going to do about it, mister?" Cole Berringer stood there with his legs slightly apart, building himself right up from the floor, Slocum noted.

"I am cutting out everything that I see has been

stolen from the Quarter Circle M. That means I'll be checking all of your stock right now, the minute I walk out of here and mount up. Do you understand me!" And Slocum, too, stood there, like he was growing right up from the floor.

"You can go plumb to hell."

"Maybe. Excepting that first I'll be cutting out those critters."

"The hell you say!" And suddenly Berringer's big palm swung out to slap his visitor in the face.

Except that Slocum's face wasn't there. Fast footwork had moved him out of harm's way.

"You son of a bitch!"

"Watch your language, Berringer."

Behind him, Slocum heard the door open and spun around to face two big men charging in. He was just in time to deliver a boot to the crotch of the man on his left, and a chopping left hook from his malletlike fist to the man at his right. Both of those guardians of Mr. Berringer's person fell in pain and fury to the floor.

"That'll do 'er! That is enough!"

It was Berringer giving that order, and he stood there while the two men got painfully to their feet.

"You two men wait outside; one of you get E.T. and tell him to wait till I'm through with Mr. Slocum here."

They were gone, covered with pain, fury, and shame.

"All right then," Berringer said. "I got your message. Set." And he nodded to an armchair.

Slocum sat down, and his host pulled over another armchair and sat facing him.

"How would you like to hire on with the Lazy CB, Slocum? I could use another ramrod. I'd make it full pay, and maybe even some extra."

Slocum wanted to grin at that, but he didn't. Suddenly he felt a liking for Berringer. The cattleman was true to his breed. A tough, hard fighter, a man who insisted on his own way—how else could the West have been won?—and a man who, though almost totally self-centered, had a streak of fairness running through him. He was the kind of man Slocum could work with, once the kinks got straightened.

They were straightened now.

"I already have a job," Slocum said. And then he added, "I appreciate the offer."

"I've heard of you, Slocum. And I see you are what you're said to be." His smile was rueful, but also careful.

"I hear tell that you've had offers to take on as sheriff since Clyde is no longer with us."

"I reckon it'd be good if one of your men was with me when I checked your stock for Quarter Circle beef. I know how easy it is on open range for stock to get mixed in together and not every rope or branding iron can always tell the difference."

"That is for sure." The rancher rose and crossed to his desk. Bending down, he opened a small cupboard door. Rising, he held a bottle in one hand, and two glasses in the other.

Slocum appreciated Berringer not asking if he wanted a drink, but simply pouring, assuming he was doing the right thing. Under other circumstances Slocum would have been tempted to refuse the drink, but he found himself cottoning to the old buzzard. He had always had a softness in him for those older men who had fought for the land and the water and their herds. He supposed that Morgan Dyce was much the same. He had at one point discussed those two former friends with Pete Mulrooney, who had known them both in the past, and still knew Cole Berringer, though not as warmly any more.

"While you get yourself around that drink there, I'd like to ask you something about how you see the situation here. Maybe it ain't my business, but then, on the other hand, maybe it is. Are you aiming to take that sheriff job? I know you bin offered. And a lot of people want you to do it. Now don't stall me off again on what I'm askin'."

"I am not a lawman," Slocum said, deciding to go along with it a little. "And anyway, I've got my hands full with the Mulrooney place."

"Hunh—"

He saw how the rancher had pushed his tongue into his cheek to make a little ball, signifying he didn't accept it all that much, but wasn't aiming to say so.

Slocum had to grin at that.

"I don't reckon you buy that too much."

"Well, I have bin told you spend a lot more time in town than you do out at the Quarter Circle M." And he nodded quickly. "Not that it's my business. But then, you know, you bin in this country a while, you got to know what's goin' on about you. You mind me?"

"I do. Man's got to watch his back trail, like they say."

"If he don't want to lose his ass, that is for sure." The rancher added his agreement and nodded vigorously.

"True enough," Slocum said. "I have been interested in what's going on, but also I am interested to find out who murdered Clyde Mulrooney." And he looked at the rancher. "You got any notions on that?"

The rancher pursed his lips, ran his palm over the

end of his nose, and squinted at his guest. "Wouldn't want to say anything directly. It is too easy to get the wrong person in trouble that way."

"It is."

"But Clyde, he was pushing on something and it could be he got too close."

"I have heard he was looking into a fellow name of Tyrone."

"Tyrone Tyrone." The cattleman nodded. "I dunno about that. And I don't know much about Tyrone, exceptin' he was said to be selling booze to the Injuns, which—well, you know what kind of trouble that can get a man into."

"And a lot of other people, too," Slocum said. "Would that be the Arapaho camp up by Franc's Fork?"

"If it's the outfit he was selling to, yeah. But that I don't know for sure. Fact, I know Rising Horse some. Had dealings with him. He is a onnery old son of a bitch, but he is all right for the matter of that. He keeps his braves on the reservation and he keeps his nose clean. Far as I know they ain't been raiding or stealing or hitting the path or anything except, like I said, keeping their nose clean."

"That doesn't mean Tyrone isn't selling something to someone, does it?"

"Man like Tyrone would sell poison to a tyke if he could make money at it. I seen the son of a bitch one time."

"And—?"

"He wasn't doing anything. He was just standing there at the First Stop Saloon in Tensleep, leaning on the bar and he just struck me as looking more or less exactly like a bucket of shit."

"I see."

"Course, I didn't like him even 'fore I met him. He is said to of killed a dog spooked his hoss; shot him, but not dead, cut off his ears while still alive. Hunh. Maybe it ain't true; on the other hand, when you take a look at that man, it is hard for you not to believe that story. You mind what I'm saying?"

"I do."

"He is selling booze to somebody, and I know just like yourself that if that gets into the hands of the Injuns there will be big trouble. There are other people worried about this, too."

"If there is so much worry over it, is anyone doing anything to see it doesn't happen?" Slocum asked. For he knew that Berringer had been building his conversation up to this point just so he could ask that question.

"I have heard that Mr. Glendenning is trying to look into the matter, that is, his council. Take that for whatever you think it means." And he lifted his glass and downed a good belt.

"I get the feeling you don't cotton too much to the council," Slocum said quietly, watching the other man carefully for a reaction.

"You take it correct, sir. I don't trust 'em far as I can throw a loaded packhorse." He ran the palm of his big hand over his face. "Exceptin' Linus. Doc, he's a good man, I will allow. But the rest, they're all followers for Glendenning."

"How come Linus is on the council then, if he's so different?"

"I figure it's on account of Glendenning wants at least one member to look good to the rest of us, so we can't say he packed the whole shebang with his own. But don't get me wrong, that Glendenning is a smart one. He could talk the drawers off a nun on Sunday morning. Slimy bugger. But he works on the quiet. Like he knows a man's weak place. That's how he's got all of them by the balls."

"All of the council?"

Berringer nodded.

"Including Linus?"

"I have a notion he does probably have something on Linus, but not so much as the others. See, Doc is a man what speaks his mind. I have heard him tell Glendenning to go piss in the wind. But he still has to foot the mark, if you get what I mean. Glendenning's smart enough not to push anybody too far. I got to admit it. He could talk a minister out of his Sunday morning take and leave the man smiling."

"Does he play poker?"

"He does. But I don't know if he does it with cards."

They both had a laugh at that.

Now a silence fell in the room while each addressed the generous drink that Berringer had poured and turned over the situation of their encounter and the gossip that had passed. Slocum still had some material he wanted to bring up.

"You mind—speaking of poker," which in fact was exactly why he had brought up the subject of gambling, "you mind that lively lady, Priscilla?"

A smile broke out on Cole Berringer's face, and Slocum had to admit it was infectious, though he kept his own face straight on purpose, not wanting to go too far in this first meeting.

"Two-Ton? She is something. She'd second deal the Devil himself just for the hell of it. I do believe it! She's got more balls than you can count in a wild herd of stud hosses. And I hope you won't make the mistake of thinking that lady has a heart of gold buried in that body."

"I am aware of that hole in the ground."

"A man just don't want to be standing in it with Priscilla about," Berringer said with a wry grin.

"On the other hand," said Slocum, "I would trust her more than most." He paused, watching the other's reaction.

The rancher was studying him from behind his glass, which was tilted to his mouth. "How so?"

"Why, I know if I was hanging over a cliff, say, holding on by my fingernails, I could trust Two-Ton to throw me a rope, but first charging me a real fair price for it!"

At that they both broke into laughter, and the conversation flowed smoothly for another ten minutes.

Then the rancher called in his foreman Ty Wills and gave instructions that would help Slocum when he was ready to separate out the beeves he found with brands that looked as though they'd been doctored.

"I hope you realize I'm giving you a damn fair deal, Slocum," Berringer said as they parted at the door.

He offered his hand and they shook on it.

"And I hope you realize I'm giving you the same," Slocum said.

8

The day had been extremely warm. The mule-drawn wagon moved slowly across the hard floor of the wide valley. It was a big wagon, and could have used more than the pair of mules to draw it, for it was heavily loaded with barrels and crates; the barrels were carrying whiskey for the various sutlers' stores in the army camps lying ahead, the bottles were for army officers in residence at the forts and outposts. The soft spring earth received the wheels of the heavy wagon deeply, leaving scars as the company of men, wagon, and mules headed toward their destination.

Two men of advanced years sat on the wagon box directly behind the mules, while a third man of equal vintage rode a short distance ahead of the team and wagon on an aged mare whose name was Mary, but was more often than not referred to by the trio as "that crowbait mare." Above this bucolic scene the sun beat down with equal intemperance on man and beast.

"Fixin' to be a short spring," the man holding the leather lines remarked. His beard, which was gray save

for the areas where it was stained auburn as a conse-
quence of frequent ejections of tobacco juice from its
owner's mouth, waggled as he spoke. He spat lazily at
the rump of one of the mules, missed, and splattered
the singletree.

"Could use me a drink, by Jesus," he muttered,
squinting at the huge sky.

"Likewise," his companion muttered.

The man up ahead on the crowbait mare said nothing. He was more or less out of earshot, anyway.

But then he spoke. "Creek up ahead." He drew his
mount back toward the wagon. "We kin let 'em blow,
and ourselves rest."

"Jesus," said the man skinning the aged team. "I am
plumb tuckered." His name was Harold O'Reilly. He
half-turned now toward the man beside him on the wagon box. "Casper, wake up. We are gettin' somewheres,
though where, who the hell knows."

"Or gives a shit," muttered Casper, still half-asleep.

"It is by God hotter'n hell in a basket," said Harold.
"If'n I sweats any more there'll be nothin' left of
me but my asshole."

"Nothin' a man can do about the weather," said the
man on horseback, falling back closer to his companions. He answered to the name Rory; no one knew
whether it was his first name or his last. "Nothing
much a man can do 'bout the weather," he repeated.

"You just said that," Harold said. "For Christ sakes!"
It angered Harold when Rory repeated himself the way
he did.

"That is what I am sayin'," Rory said. "The fuckin'
weather drives a man off his head."

"That's all there is out here on this godforsaken
prairie anyways," said Casper, coming to a little more.

Silence now fell upon the trio and their beasts of burden as they approached the shade of the trees lining the creek. Drawing rein, Harold brought the mule team to a stop. He sighed.

It was definitely cooler in the shade, near the creek, without the glare in their eyes. Harold wrapped the lines around the brake handle and then stepped down stiffly from the wagon box. Casper was already on the ground, and Rory dismounted the mare.

The three moved closer to the creek, which was lined with willows and cottonwoods. They all carried weapons: side arms and Henry rifles. They were old hands at packing whiskey from the Union Pacific tracks, south of Tensleep, up to the pass in the Big Horn Range at Thumb Gap. Almost invariably the trip had been routine, nothing but the heat or, depending on the time of year, the cold being their main problem.

There had been brief skirmishes with the tribes, but nothing serious. The hostiles were easily paid off with beef or booze. The shipment, principally whiskey, was artfully camouflaged with beef, giving the appearance that meat was their main cargo. Then, when a drink or so was offered, in goodwill, there was no problem. At the same time, the knowledge that the army outpost was not far away helped their passage most certainly. And so it was the usual thing to pay off their possible attackers with merchandise, of which they had plenty. Sometimes even parting with a bottle or two, reluctantly to be sure, but wisely nonetheless.

Now, relaxing in the shade, with an ample serving of liquid refreshment, the three had spread a blanket upon which a card game, jacks or better, was just getting warmed up.

"We just got to remember not to forget meetin' up

with Tyrone," Harold said, putting the statement out in the manner of a man who is saying it not in order to remember it, but to forget it. Indeed, his companions heard the words, but their attention was definitely on more important matters: the game, and the satisfying beverage which supported them in their difficult journey of delivering their precious cargo.

Indeed, so wrapped in their pleasure, the three failed to hear the approach of their visitors until it was far too late. They had no time to even touch their weapons before the painted, shrieking redskins were upon them.

News of the "massacre" reached town before the day was done. Except that it wasn't, in fact, anything of the sort. The three had not been killed. They were still alive, though roughed up considerably, and scared almost completely out of even the possibility of giving an intelligent account of what had happened. Indeed, they were physically unscathed, sound in body if not in mentality or emotion.

Riders from a neighboring ranch, Clem Asher's Double Fork on Bucket Creek, had discovered the three lying unconscious in the midst of chaos.

The two riders had first thought the men had drunk themselves into oblivion, but after seeing the condition of the packing cases and wagons, realized that theft had taken place. Also, the mules had been arrowed to death. Yet the three were snoring away as though sleeping off a celebration. Closer examination, however, revealed the fact that stern blows had been delivered to render them unconscious, though not dead.

It was clear to the line riders, Phil Octo and his brother Brad, that whiskey had been the purpose for the

Indian attack. In fact, a couple of bottles had been dropped during the melee, and their contents still scented the atmosphere.

Not far from the discovery of the battered oldsters, their dead, philosophical mules, and their vanished treasure, a lone rider drew rein on the crest of a long coulee and surveyed the scene.

John Slocum had been out tallying the Berringer stock as well as looking for anything that might have been slipped over from the Quarter Circle M brand.

The scene below looked like what it was, and the closer he got to the tableau which now included the two dismounted riders from the Double Fork, the more he realized how bad the news not only was but was going to get.

The two men looked up at him as he drew rein and stepped down from the Appaloosa.

"Mornin'." One of them nodded. The other kept on examining some prints near where the three men were still lying, though they were now recovering, thanks to water brought to them by their rescuers.

"They was about a hunnert of the red devils!" said Harold swiftly. He was holding his head; he'd been cut above the eye, and he was also dealing with a big pain in his side.

Rory had also been cut, alongside the jaw, and had been smashed in the ear. While Casper, the third member of the trio, had been kicked in the crotch and was cursing and holding himself, though his curses were necessarily muted due to the vulnerability of the area that had been attacked.

"Don't look to be a hunnert," said Phil Octo, and his tone was decisive. "Judgin' by these here prints."

"A hunnert," Harold repeated.

"Easy that," Rory said. "Mebbe more even. They was all over the place, screamin' an' swarmin' and like. God, the red devils!"

"They have hit the path," said Casper. "And that is for sure!"

"Not that much tracks," claimed Phil Octo, and he looked over at his brother, who partly out of sight of the three victims of the "massacre" tapped his finger in the direction of his head and crossed his eyes.

"You boys wasn't here," Rory said. "Or you'd be talkin' otherwise, by damn!" And he spat angrily at nowhere in particular.

Slocum by now was also studying the prints of the horses and the men.

"What tribe?" he asked the trio. "You have any idea?"

"Dunno," said Casper. "They was so many and they come so fast a man didn't have time even to scratch hisself 'fore they was right on top of us!"

"I'd reckon a dozen give or take," one of the Double Fork riders said. It was Phil Octo.

His brother Brad nodded.

Slocum said, "And they took the whiskey, that it?" He was standing next to the survivors, who were recovering at a fair pace, though their agitation was still trying to overcome the fact that it was all right now to be calm and to take it slow.

Slocum had picked up one of the arrows that was lying on the ground.

"This arrow is Sioux," he said. "And that arrow yonder is Shoshone."

The two Octo brothers had suddenly stopped and turned toward him. "What are you saying there, mister?"

"And that coup stick lying there has no reason to be there. Under what we're reading here, they didn't have to be in any hurry to pull out. And besides, they wouldn't have left that coup stick. Not like that."

"Are you sayin' what I'm thinking?" Brad Octo said.

"I'm sayin' that I lay odds they were whites dressed up as Indian and not knowing much, if anything, about the tribes."

"We'll be getting back to the Double Fork," Phil Octo said. "Clem'll want to know about this." He turned to the three. "You men can come along with us, if you've a mind to."

"I'll be headin' into town," Slocum said.

"You'll let 'em know in town, will you?" Brad Octo said.

"That is what I was figurin' to do," Slocum said.

Harold was standing now. "We oughtta be gettin' to town, exceptin' myself, I don't want another such attack. I don't give a shit whether they're red or white, the sons of bitches not only bashed us up, they took all that whiskey; goddamn their eyes!"

"Boss can likely send you into town in the buckboard," Brad Octo said. And he looked at his brother, who nodded in agreement.

"We'll do 'er like that way then," Harold said. And his two companions looked at him, Casper nodding his head once, and Rory scratching his crotch.

The lengthening light seemed to touch everywhere in the little town, changing each window, door, house, the bit and bridle on the roan horse at the hitching rail outside Miller's General Store, the ring on Mrs. Ohrwasher's hand as she took down her laundry from the line in back of her house, the gold tooth in Country McCloskey's mouth as he grinned at one of Louise's girls seated in the window of her crib down the street from Two-Ton Priscilla's place in Skintown. The darkening light washed over the entire town, touching everyone's mood and reaching toward the evening, which even before being spoken of, was already the night.

Thus Slocum arrived on the Appaloosa, melting into the night scene as though he'd never been away. And for the matter of that, it was the way he liked it.

He did not like at all the way things were moving toward himself as a possible—no, likely—center of action. It was not his concern. He didn't know what was going on, though he did have his suspicions, and he didn't know who was running the game, though he had a good notion. Yes, there was Clyde Mulrooney still in the picture, as good a man as he'd ever ridden with; and he would like to help his family and his memory in any way that he possibly could. But he did not like messing in other people's lives. Like messing around a broomtail's rear end, a man could get his head kicked off, or worse.

Still, there was Alison, or Ali as everybody called her. Her freshness, the way her eyes lit when she saw him, not to overlook the way she made love made her special, and that word was a weak one.

And there was Doc Linus: gentle, tough, kind, cynical, and a smart aleck to boot. He was everything. But the man had lived a full life or two in that adventure with his girl and his trying to save her life. And the man was caught. Glendenning had him by the balls, as indeed it seemed more and more he had the town, or at least the principal individuals, which was where the power counted.

What did Glendenning want? The town? Well, he had it, in effect, but evidently he wanted more. He wanted to be known. The man surely wanted even more power: the county, the territory, maybe even a move to Washington. It was clear that he was working with the railroad, which actually meant that he was working off the Union Pacific, using them for his own gain. As he was using the council. But he was still behind the scenes, even though people spoke of him as a power. He still had not yet taken the stage. And Slocum was sure that almost any moment now, he would. With all the action of Tyrone Tyrone's whiskey dealing, with Morgan Dyce driving his herd north to ship out of Eagle Pass when he could more easily have chosen any of three or four other places nearer to his base.

And where did all this leave Cole Berringer? Somehow Slocum felt that Berringer was not as concerned with Dyce as Dyce was with Berringer. And, too, if Dyce was working with Glendenning, well, it was common knowledge that Glendenning, or at any rate the railroad, had offered to buy the Lazy CB. That range was right in the way of a line from Ulysses to the north, through Wind City to the southwest, with a spur that could be added for Eagle Pass.

Much of this information Slocum had gleaned from talking to various people, picking up bits and pieces, and knitting them together in a fresh pattern. People such as Pete Mulrooney Doc Linus, and Two-Ton Priscilla independently of each other had revealed pieces of the pattern that added up to a plum waiting for the plucking. And even the raiding of one of Tyrone Tyrone's whiskey wagons, allegedly by Indians, added support to this suggestion: that it was all part of a larger pattern, at the center of which was Arthur Glendenning,

backed by the railroad and very likely powers back
East.

With this slant in mind, it was easy enough to see how
all the players—Doc, Morgan Dyce, Cole Berringer, the
council members, Two-Ton Priscilla, the whole damn
town in fact—were involved. Divide and conquer.
Where had he heard that? It didn't matter. He was
seeing it, right in front of him. And right now, swift
as a whistle in a windstorm, he admonished himself to
watch his back. Or by God, he'd be getting it, too. He
grinned at himself at that. But he felt better than he
had in a long while. It was beginning to fit together
so a man could see what he'd been looking at all this
time without actually seeing much of anything.

In the room at the back of Two-Ton Priscilla's, the
mood was optimistic; the atmosphere was heavy, however, with the smoke from Tyrone Tyrone's pipe. And
Arthur Glendenning, to his chagrin, had found that his
own expensive Havana cigar did little to modify the air
in these close quarters. Nevertheless, he was a man of
principle, and he stayed with his decision to conclude
a successful meeting with the knobby little Irishman,
whose nickname, a relic from his early days in the
bare-knuckle prize ring, was Stonehead.

"I tell ye," Stonehead Tyrone was saying, "I don't
favor the dee-struction of all that booze, even though
you sez the end justifies the means. That's a helluva
lot of good whiskey down the pipe, and money to
boot!" He nodded, winking in support of the finality
of his statement, and drew on his short pipe, which
was almost hidden in the great knuckles of his fist.

"As I say, it was necessary," Glendenning replied
smoothly, smiling gently at the other man, moving

his hand about, as he held his cigar, in expansive gestures.

"The thing is, me boy, we don't want the army jumpin' up our arse."

"Of course." Glendenning beamed. He'd been anticipating the point. "For sure. But they won't. I mean, they won't so long as we maintain our contract. After all, the army people do very well by your business, Tyrone."

"That I know."

"It would only be a problem if some idiot decided on some kind of holy crusade against the demon rum. That sort of thing."

"I know, I know. I know there is that kind of insanity about during times of stress."

"The point is for the whiskey not to get into the hands of the tribes. We know that that is—well, dynamite." Glendenning spread his hands. "There's of course no reason why it should."

"The attack—"

"That was not Indians. It was whites. Men from, well, from a source at my disposal."

"But the army will hear of it."

"Precisely." Glendenning was smiling like a chess player who foresees his master stroke several moves ahead. "Of course," he said again. "But you see, my friend, that is precisely what will stir the town and its environs to accept the need for a strong council to protect them, to administer in such a way that such Indian uprisings will not occur again. I'm sure you understand me."

"That I do, lad. That I do." Tyrone Tyrone lowered his bushy gray-white eyebrows so that his laughing eyes disappeared for a moment as he nodded wisely, chuckling deep in his chest and throat, and then lowering one lid over an eye to ensure the mutual understanding upon which the enterprise was built.

"Then we'll continue with the same route, is that it?" The Irishman's eyebrows lifted in query.

"Not quite the same, for we must beware of prying eyes. The army, as we know, is not above such maneuvers as spying on the citizenry. On the other hand, they are also always strapped for funds and equipment, not to mention in a number of cases, intelligence. All the same, you cannot count on those kinds of windfalls. One has to plan for any and every contingency." He beamed. "Wouldn't you say?"

"I say that's quite a mouthful," replied Stonehead Tyrone. His brogue was especially heavy as he voiced this, for he was always a man with a sense of humor, and nothing delighted him more than to "spoke" somebody of the "Fancy Dan" society, such as he saw Arthur Glendenning to be.

Glendenning knew this, but since money and power were stronger goals than even self-esteem, he did not demean himself by putting the Irisher down. He simply let his thoughts do what wisely he witheld from his mouth.

"The one we have to keep our eye on, of course, is this man Slocum." Glendenning raised his glass, readying it for a toast, and looked at his companion over its top.

"To our—uh—effort," he said. "No, let me change that." He paused, lowering the glass just slightly and then saying, "To our success. Our great success!"

"I'll drink to that!" The great fist closed on its glass of whiskey.

Together they downed their drinks.

"You'll be in town tomorrow for the election," Glendenning said, watching his companion.

"I don't believe in that voting business," Tyrone said.

"But if it helps our cause—"

"Then that's a horse of a different color!"

"Well put," Glendenning said as they both rose to their feet.

Later, in another part of town, the plan was embellished upon. The Eagle Pass Council, to use their own assumed nomenclature, sat variously in the office of Arthur Glendenning. That is to say, two extra chairs and a stool had been brought in to augment the office furniture. Arthur Glendenning believed in simplicity in relation to business. Thus, there was customarily his own desk chair, and one chair for one visitor. Now the four members sat in a semicircle facing their host and accepted leader.

"It is, of course, Slocum we have still to be careful about," Glendenning was telling them. "He has been checking on Berringer's stock, claiming that brands have been reworked, and all in all has been helping with the Mulrooney Quarter Circle M as a sort of acting foreman. We know he has visited Berringer personally, though I doubt he got very far with that gentleman, any more than he would with Morgan Dyce. I think we can count on those two knocking each other out of the picture."

"Dyce and Berringer," someone said in a low voice.

"But of course." Glendenning regarded Homer Content sourly. "That's who we're talking about, Homer." He raised his voice. "We must pay close attention now."

And it was as though a schoolroom had suddenly shuffled into a half-gloomy obedience. Doc was sitting on the stool and continued to slouch, however, even though he wanted to straighten up. The point was, he didn't like Glendenning; the point was he found himself disgusted by the man. But his companions were all sitting as though interested and listening well.

"We have to be careful that the army doesn't get the notion of imposing martial law, for one thing. For another, we do not want any trouble whatsoever with the Arapaho, especially Rising Horse's band. And Slocum. Again, and always, there is this man to be reckoned with. I believe we are getting close to the place where—"

"No!"

The room came to a stop as though someone had fired a pistol. It was Doc Linus who had spoken, and now he was sitting upright on his stool, leaning a little forward, with his face earnest, even hard, as he said, "I will not go along with any action that, well, tries or succeeds in injuring or killing Slocum."

"But, Sophocles—Sophocles, I was only going to suggest that he be watched."

"You already have men watching him. You said so earlier."

"But a bit more closely. And look, it wouldn't hurt to warn him off with a little roughing up." Glendenning was leaning forward in his chair with an earnest look on his face, first regarding Doc Linus, then looking at each of the others in turn.

"I don't think John Slocum is the kind of man who would be intimidated by roughing up."

"But he might."

"You mean, with perhaps a dozen or so bullies with

clubs and a few other persuaders. Boy oh boy!" Doc shook his head in disgust.

"But Sophocles, not if you disagree." Contrition seemed to appear in every inch of Arthur Glendenning's body.

Suddenly Linus changed his approach. "Do what you like," he said, offhand. "Please yourselves. Slocum will be what he is, and we will be what we are. And whatever is going to happen will happen. In the long run, we're all headed for the same place. And so—" He shrugged, opening his hands in a helpless gesture.

"We can see," said Glendenning. "We can see." His tone was almost unctious as he looked slightly hurt by Linus's words, words that he clearly took as a betrayal. But being big about it, he was pardoning.

A short silence followed, during which Homer Content, who owned the Enterprise, the hotel where they were meeting, rose and went out to relieve himself, and also to stretch his legs.

During his absence nobody said anything, but they all roused themselves when there was a knock at the door and it turned out to be a barman with refreshments.

"Aah," sighed Glendenning. "Homer knows how to play the host."

They drank in less solemnity now, and when Homer returned, the group agreed with Glendenning's suggestion that an election be run as soon as possible in order to fortify their own position by changing from "acting council" to "council."

Nobody objected, not even Sophe Linus. It was agreed that plans for the election would begin on the next day, and that since it was nearly the Fourth of July, that would be the most likely day for the event.

9

In Two-Ton Priscilla's Premier Saloon Drinking and Eating Emporium, John Slocum again ran into a familiar face—and figure. It was on these lively premises that he had first met the fabulous Nellie, and running into her once more was a happy moment. He had stopped by principally to see if he could catch any gossip on how the town was reacting to the "Indian attack" on the illegal whiskey wagon.

As always, the barroom was crowded, the gaming tables were filled, men stood "cheek-by-jowel" as the editor of the *Rocky Mountain Trumpet* had so frequently put it, and the girls, also described in newspaper jargon as "Cyprians," "fallen doves," or ladies of pleasure, were also plying their wares. All of this activity was covered by thick smoke, noise, and a tempo of activity that would certainly have forbidden anything on the order of serious reflection.

Slocum simply allowed himself to become a part of the lively scene. Early on he had noted that he was being watched; mostly by two men, who lounged at opposite ends of the room. There could have been others, he knew. Nor was he surprised. Things were coming to a point and he had known for some while during the past few days that he was under surveillance. He didn't mind; it was what he expected, and it had the merit of showing him that certain people were concerned over his presence in Eagle Pass, and that therefore more was afoot than met a first look.

What he hadn't expected, on the other hand, was the delightful surprise of running into Nellie. Even realizing that she worked the premises, he still hadn't had her in the front of his mind, and the surprise made the meeting more delightful.

"I missed you," she said.

"Likewise." He grinned at her, taking in her exquisite bosom, a good area of which was not covered by her clothing.

"Hah! I'll bet," she said, and added, "Mr. Stranger!"

"I'll bet, too," he said, playing it straight.

"I'm only funning you," she said. "It just felt like a long time, is all."

"Well, it might be good fun to feel for a long time," he said, brushing his arm against her as they walked to a table that had just been vacated.

"The trouble with you is you're so good-looking," she said, and sat down while the young bartender who was helping out brought drinks.

"You look pretty good yourself," he said.

For a moment they were silent. He watched her fingering her glass, as though she was thinking about something.

"I know they're watching me," he said.

"You were reading my mind." She kept her eyes down on her hands as she spoke. "They've got men spotting you all around town, I have heard. Did you know that?" And she raised her eyes to look at him.

"I've noticed something in the way of a welcome to Eagle Pass since the moment I rode in," he said. "Where does that leave you?"

"Right where I am now." She lifted her glass, holding it as if for a toast. "I'm the bait, I guess."

"Best bait I've ever run into, miss. But I'd best like to have you out of the way."

She shrugged. "Too late, my friend. I'm here. They want me to soften you up, I guess."

"Except that right now I'm pretty hard."

"We'd better not go upstairs. They'll get you with your pants down."

"Funny. That's just the way I want to get you."

She leaned toward him, her eyes on her drink which she was holding between her hands. "Listen, be serious. These men are not playing. It's for sure. They're hired. They don't know you from a dry well. They'd as soon kill you, beat you up, as spit on a pissant."

"You're not telling me anything I don't know."

"Then be serious."

"All right. I will. Tell me, have they got anything on you? I mean, any score?"

"Only I happened to be here, working for Priscilla."

"Did Two-Ton set you up for this?"

"No. Priscilla isn't that way. She had nothing to do with it. Someone must have found out that we got together, so they decided to use it if they could."

"I want you to get up and go on up to your room upstairs," Slocum said.

"And what are you going to be doing?"

"I'll be here seeing just what happens."

"I don't think I want to do that," she said, and he

heard how she caught her breath as she spoke.

"I want you to."

"But what about you?"

"I thought I might have a conversation with one of those sweet gentlemen, and I don't want you to get caught up in any donnybrook."

"I want to stay here," she insisted. "Please. And besides," she added swiftly as he started to interrupt. "I happen to have something here in my handbag that might be useful. I am referring to that invention by, I think it was a French gent, name of Henry Deringer."

He looked into her eyes then and saw nothing but a blue wall.

"Good enough then," he said after a short pause and, pushing back his chair, he stood up, taking his half-filled glass with him.

He could feel the eyes on him as he walked to the bar and ordered another drink. He had chosen one end of the bar where a big, thick-shouldered man with a broken nose was standing, with his thick fingers loosely around his glass of beer as he leaned on the bar. Slocum was keeping his attention also in the big mirror so that he could see most of the rest of the room.

"You tryin' to push in here, mister?" the big man said as Slocum's arm brushed his.

There was a smile on Slocum's face, which should have warned the other man, but didn't. "Just trying to get myself a place here." He started to back off, but then suddenly moved in close, bringing his knee up into the other man's crotch. In the next second he had spun away and brought a chopping punch down onto the back of the other man's neck as he bent over in pain from the blow to his manhood.

And because of the mirror, Slocum was ready for

the man who was standing beside the one who was now sagging in agony to the floor. Just in the nick of time he slipped away from the haymaker that had been aimed at his jaw and slammed a wicked right hook into the attacker's heart. The would-be convincer let out a gasp of agony and sank to the floor.

Meanwhile, a circle had formed around the three combatants, while at the same time the other side of the room had become activated as someone drew a gun, but was slammed in the jaw by someone else. Immediately, the entire barroom was in a turmoil, as everyone seemed to be fighting everyone else.

However, Slocum could not afford to be distracted by this remarkable scene. A fat man suddenly dove at his legs and another aimed a whistling punch at his head. A knee took care of the diver, and his elbow cracked the man who tried to punch him, landing right on his attacker's ear and dropping him like a lump of wet laundry. Slocum stepped over him just as the entire room erupted in violence. A chair flung at him grazed his back, and since he was off balance, he went down. Now, everyone was throwing punches or furniture at everyone else. The bartender was shouting for order, but to no avail. He had been searching for his bung starter and now finally found it and began laying about until he was brought to his knees by a flying jug.

Meanwhile the big door into the dancing room was thrown open and the fiddlers, horn player, and drummer all entered, breaking into a solemn rendition of "The Star Spangled Banner" as at the same instant Two-Ton Priscilla's voice covered everything within sound and sight as she sang: "Oh, say can you see . . ."

One man was instantly transfixed into a statue of patriotism as he stood stock-still in the center of the free-

for-all, rigidly responding to the call of his country, but
only for a moment, until a drunken cowpoke slammed
him over the head with a bottle and he went down in a
splatter of glass, alcohol, and blood. His assailant was
immediately brought down with a flying chair that swept
the bottles and glasses from an empty table, and finally
ended up targeting an innocent spittoon that had been
randomly kicked away from the bar when the fracas
began.

Slocum had by now fought his way across the room
to where Nellie was standing against the wall. The
four men who had been watching him had all been
accounted for; three by Slocum, the fourth by a flying
chair that had smashed into his lower back, bringing
him into the middle of what a moment ago had been a
poker game. He had landed on the table, with money,
cards, chips, and drinks flying in all directions. One
of the card players—evidently the one who'd been
winning—underlined the fallen man's misfortune by
pounding him in the back of the neck with his fist
which was still holding his winning hand.

Nellie had received a slight cut from flying glass
along the back of her hand. Slocum's knuckles were
bruised, his ear hurt, and he was experiencing what
would surely become a pretty big bruise along his ribs.
But it seemed nothing was broken.

"I'm worried about Priscilla," Nellie said when they
reached his room. "I owe her; she's always been square
with me."

"Two-Ton can handle herself," Slocum said. "Didn't
you see her two gunmen covering the room while all
the action was going on?"

"Why, no." And then, "But why didn't they stop
it?"

"I figure on account of Two-Ton wanted the chance to sing her head off. What the hell, we won't know if everything'll settle down now on account of everybody wearing themselves out, or on account of the power of Two-Ton's singing. What do you think, miss?"

She was already laughing before he finished. "I know what you mean," she said, drying her eyes. "Priscilla—Two-Ton—is the kind of person who can talk herself out of a lynching by arguing with the vigilantes that they didn't tie the knot the way it's supposed to be."

They laughed at that, and then Slocum said, "Let's get the rest of your clothes untied, miss. I don't care what kind of knots you've been using, so long as they pull loose."

They had moved the herd when the feed at Crazy Wolf Crossing gave out after holding those beeves there for so long a time. But Morgan Dyce was playing his hand carefully. In no way did he trust Cole Berringer, yet he was stuck for his market if he didn't go along. The news that had reached him in the first place down below the Cimarron, which had changed his mind for him and brought him to Eagle Pass, had been that his regular market was all but glutted. For a fact, he'd heard, the whole damn beef market was fixing to bust. He didn't regret his decision, but he hadn't exactly figured on busting into Berringer.

A few of the boys had slipped into town while they'd been holding the herd at Crazy Wolf Crossing and the news they'd brought back wasn't good.

He figured that Berringer was in the middle of it, but that the railroad also had its hooks out. It wasn't a good situation for him and his cows, but he was in no position to be choosey. He figured it would have

been worse to head for Ellsworth or Abilene or one
of the regular places. There was still that rankling
and rasping in him. Fifteen years hadn't lost him any
of the bitterness and, on some nights, the anger. By
God, he was thinking, he'd been pretty damn nice to
that bullheaded son of a bitch. Who the hell did he
think he was, sending him a message he wanted to
see him. Pretending like everything was all jake and
forgiven now, and they'd maybe work together to help
get the town straightened out. What had he said? "Us
two cattlemen what's bin here since the beginning of
things, we oughtta stick together, not let the railroads
and merchants and all those back-East people come on
in here and take over everything."

Well, the old bugger was right. But it wasn't Dyce's
fault that Berringer happened to be right. He just
happened to be thinking some good sense for a change,
by accident.

Of course it was true that he and Berringer were just
about the only old-timers left. In fact, they were the
last. He had checked on that, as he had on a few other
things since he'd been up in this northern country. He'd
sent E.T. into town a lot, and a couple of others he'd
trusted, and a couple he didn't trust, too, men such as
that pair of hot guns, Honniger and Deltus.

The situation was pretty much what he'd figured
out by himself. Greedy merchants, greedy railroad,
everybody wanting to take over. The merchants wanted
law and order, too, but law and order under the gun;
with old Clyde Mulrooney gone, that was the size of
it. And then the easterners coming in, like that one
Cole had mentioned, Glen something. Then, wouldn't
you know, the man comes out for a visit. Glen—
Glendenning, that was it. Funny monicker. And a face

he wouldn't trust as far as he could spit in a Kansas twister. Glen Denning. Two names? Or was it one? Didn't matter. The feller was a crook. You could smell him a mile away and you didn't even have to be downwind.

Dyce had wanted to check in with Berringer, too, since they were the last of the old stock who opened the country. So, he'd gone along. It hadn't cost him anything. And he'd take a hand in the game, till he'd see it was gonna cost him and then he'd toss it in. The hell with it! He was going to go along, but playing his own hand the while. Did those idiots Berringer and Glen think he was a fool?

Then this feller Slocum. He was hearing a good bit about this man from Deltus and Honniger. They knew about him. Slocum was fast with the gun. And he was tough. He'd heard something or other about him in the past, but he couldn't recollect just what it was. Something about Quantrill? The name kept coming in. Quantrill. Slocum had ridden with him or against him; he wasn't sure which he'd heard. At any event, Slocum was said to be one tough son of a bitch and no man to mess with. Well, by God, neither was he. Neither was Morgan Dyce a man to mess with.

He was standing there by the thin morning cook fire as Honniger and Deltus rode in. The sun wasn't all the way up, but the sky was light in the east, and all the rest of it was clear.

Morgan Dyce squinted up at the two riders as they drew rein and nodded at him. He did not return the nod.

"Town still there?"

The one named Honniger nodded. "It is. Though some of it got lost in the action at that place run by the woman."

"Woman?"

"A woman name of Priscilla Two-Ton," said his companion, Deltus.

"It is Two-Ton Priscilla," Honniger said.

"Makes no different," Deltus said. "There was a lot of fighting. A helluva lot, and that feller Slocum, he begun it."

"What about?" Morgan Dyce canted his head to one side as the men sat their horses. He had not told them to get down and since they had done so once before without being asked by their boss, they had learned, and remained mounted.

"Looked to be Slocum started it, exceptin' maybe it was somethin' one feller said, but we didn't hear it."

"They're layin' for him is what you're sayin'."

"It looks to be that."

"Berringer's men?"

"Dunno," Deltus said. "Nobody seemed to know. And it wasn't right to ask too close."

"There was Berringer men there," Honniger said. "Could tell by their talkin'. But they might of not started it. Could of been Slocum hisself."

"You talk to anybody? Any Berringer men?"

"Nope." Honniger shook his head. "They had that big fat woman there singin'."

"I'm askin' about who you talked with, or what you heard." Morgan Dyce had started building himself a cigarette then, and he had his head canted forward, but he still had his attention on what was going on around him.

"What you figger, E.T.?" he said now, without looking up as his ramrod, E. T. Crimmins, approached.

Deltus and Honniger exchanged swift glances of careful surprise at the way the head of the Double

Back D had known of the arrival of his foreman who, as far as either of them could tell, hadn't made a sound. And you couldn't smell him, plus Dyce by God had his back to him.

E.T. didn't seem surprised, but then he'd be used to such a man. The two gunmen looked at each other, and some kind of message passed between them. Neither one knew what it was except maybe to watch it, with a man like that.

"I heerd Pete Mulrooney stole his brother's body and buried it someplace nobody knows where," the ramrod said.

"Anybody throw a objection at that?" Dyce said, looking up now, canting his head at the foreman.

"Not that I heard of it."

"What do you hear of Slocum?"

"I hear he is one tough son of a bitch and he can draw and fire that six-gun of his quicker'n a scared cat can piss."

"Hunh—"

"That is for sure." The foreman reached up with his thick forefinger and pushed back his wide-brimmed hat. He had the sun in his eyes then, so he had to squint. "Other than that he 'pears to be a man keeps his nose clean. I reckon you all heard about Tyrone's whiskey wagon and the Injun attack."

Morgan Dyce didn't answer, he just stood there looking at the pair of gunmen who got the message and turned their horses without a word and rode off to the corral.

"I heerd," Dyce said. "What d'you make of that?"

"Well, they tried to make it look like a Injun attack, exceptin' they left so many mistakes about, it fooled nobody. Slocum was the one cottoned to it. He is a smart one, Morg. He even suggested it might have been Injuns pretendin' not to be Injuns, but then dropped that, and he was right. It was whites."

"Know who?"

The foreman shook his head. " 'Pears it was a put-up job to scare folks."

"What folks?" Dyce spat quickly and then stood up straighter and squared his shoulders. He had a pain in his back from having been not too well seated the day before when he'd roped a wild calf from a pony he'd only just broke.

"Folks around," E.T. said. "Somebody—more'n likely Tyrone—is running whiskey to the tribes. And somebody wants folks to get angried up about it. Somethin' like that. Hell, I dunno. You ast me what the talk was. That's the size of it."

They were both silent then. Dyce had built his smoke, had lit it, and was squinting into the sunrise above the high peaks he was facing.

"You got any word from Berringer?"

His foreman nodded.

"He says start 'em in tomorrer."

"Tomorrow, huh? About time."

A silence fell between them now. And it lengthened, while neither one made a move to speak or to walk away.

Finally E.T. said, "I hear the town is planning their election for tomorrer," he said.

"Why?"

"They said on account of it's the Fourth of July."

Morgan Dyce spat, stood there swing-hipped, with his hands stuck into his rear pants pockets, his cigarette hanging easy on his lower lip, squinting into the sun.

He continued to stand just like that as his foreman

walked off, heading for the campfire.

Presently, he felt the dog near him, and looking down, he saw him sitting on his haunches looking toward the rising sun. The dog, who had three legs—the left foreleg having been lost during a cattle stampede—stood up and came over to sniff at something in a clump of sage near where the boss of the Double Back D was standing.

"Well, Tip, you son of a bitch, what we gonna do?"

But Tip ignored him. He was pretty damn wild, everyone knew, but he was also about the best cattle dog you could find. Rare, they were. Running horses was not like running the goddamn woolies. Tip was tough, and the horses respected him. So did the men. A dog who did his job and minded himself. Worth more than any two men, Morgan Dyce was thinking. And he didn't come hanging around like a lot of dogs— and people—did. Kept himself to himself. Like a dog ought to. And a man, too. These hands you get to hire nowadays—all soft, all wanting something extra. A man, well, these days a man was rare. Like Tip there. He remembered that stampede. That big sorrel stallion had kicked Tip in the leg. Finally, they'd had to cut it off. Dyce had done it himself. The dog had fought him, but he'd done it and washed the wound with whiskey, and by God somehow old Tip had pulled through. Had to! They were all the hell and gone from any camp or town with a sawbones. And by damn that dog had pulled through and he'd gone on rounding up horses on three legs. By damn, he could probably do it on two, if he ever had to.

And now Dyce, who was getting on and was no longer young, and the dog, also older and minus something of what he once had, but maybe now having more of something else, like the man, stayed right where they were watching the sun moving higher into the sky and the sky lightening and the smell of the fresh new day arriving, along with the strong smell of sage and pine and the cattle and the horses. All the smells and the little and big sounds of daily life.

Tomorrow Morgan Dyce was going to drive his herd into the town's stockyards and meet the agent and get his money. And then he was going to head back to Texas. He hadn't really wanted to bring his herd here to Eagle Pass. He hadn't yet visited the town for the same reason. She wouldn't be there, he knew. And yet, at the same time, there would be something of her there. And he wasn't looking forward to that. Yet at the same time, he was. He looked over to see Tip, but the dog was no longer there.

10

Even before going out into the street, Slocum could feel the difference in this particular day. Looking down from the window of the girl's room, he could sense the anticipation that was in the air. And though he'd enjoyed himself immensely in bed with his companion, he found his thoughts moving toward Alison Mulrooney. Alison was special, though that was taking nothing away from his friend Nellie. Still, Slocum's thoughts were on the young girl out at the Quarter Circle M.

"It's going to be a tough day," he said, coming back.

Nellie, half uncovered, stretched her full length on the bed. "You're expecting trouble?"

"I am. I think you'd better stay close to yourself today."

She sat up now, but held the sheet over her breasts. "I can tell you really mean that," she said.

"I do. Stay indoors as much as you can; in fact, stay inside all day. Don't go out."

"You're leaving now?"

"Sorry."

"No. No, I didn't mean it like that. I know you have to go. I wasn't trying to keep you."

He stood by the bed, looking down at her. And as she looked up at him, he thought her blue eyes—indeed, her whole attitude—looked wistful.

"Is there anything I can do?" she asked.

"There is. You can do something very important for me."

"Tell."

"Stay alert. Don't go out into the street."

"It's the Fourth of July today. Everyone will be in the street. They'll be celebrating. Firecrackers and singing and dancing and all like that. It will be fun."

"It might not just be firecrackers," he said. And now he was stern. "You asked if there was something you could do. I just told you."

Her face suddenly changed. There was an expression now that he had not seen before. "I want you to do something for me then. All right? Fair exchange?"

"I wish we could, but—"

"I wasn't asking you that, dammit. Didn't you get enough when we woke up just—what?—less than an hour ago. And twice last night!" And she was laughing, though he heard a nervousness in it.

He grinned at her. "Sorry."

"Don't be sorry."

"Actually, I'm glad."

"Glad! Well, I'll be—"

"Glad you're still thinking about it," he said, and he sat down on the edge of the bed and put his arm around her.

It was a long kiss, a sweet kiss. And they both clung to it.

Then he said as he stood up, "I wish it was that kind of day, but it isn't."

"It isn't for me, either," she said.

He walked to the door. "See ya."

"You know, if I can help—"

"I know," he said. "And you know, if you—"

"I do," she said, cutting in.

And that was how they left it. She was sitting up in the bed, with only her bare arms showing, and her smile and big blue eyes.

"Come back soon," she said. "That's what I wanted you to do for me."

"I will."

When he got downstairs and walked out into the street, he felt the cool of the early morning on his bare hands and face. He had already checked his weapons, and now he turned his steps in the direction of the livery. He'd fork some hay for the Appaloosa and pour some oats, then he'd get himself outside a steak and potatoes and a couple of mugs of coffee.

For the moment, that was what was necessary. The rest would follow in its own time. Wherever or whatever, he would be where it was. He would be here.

As the light of the morning sun began to wash over the town, it also invaded the office of Arthur Glendenning, who, as always, was up early. He had two reasons for rising early: one, because he found the early hours conducive to his private work, thoughts, plans, and his particular hobby; the other was simply that he was not able to sleep late. And he felt himself fortunate in this, for he was able to give himself to the practice of his secret ambition.

This endeavor he usually exercised some distance

outside of town, in a special place he'd discovered where, thus far at any rate, he had been undisturbed. Yet this particular morning, because of the nature of the activities which were about to unfold and of which he was one of the principal authors, he remained in his house, practicing his hobby simply by studying the speed of his draw.

A full mirror enabled him to study his moves as he stood relaxed, ready, facing himself; then he let his hand sweep to the Navy Colt in a dry draw. He tried this exercise a number of times. Then turned his back to the mirror, and tried with a turn. Not so simple, that one. But he was trying. And he knew that practice makes perfect, or at any rate, he knew it was supposed to.

Today, he was filled with another excitement, however, and it took him a while to get steady. He was tense. And he accepted this fact, for he knew he had good reason to be tense. Everything depended on this day. Everything! He had bullied, chivied and chiseled, smoothed and stroked his way with lies, charm, cheating, flattery, and even telling the truth. Selling himself not only to the Devil, as he expressed it to himself, but even to God, when it proved beneficial. In this sense, he might in a measure be called an honest man, for he knew who and what he was.

Thus he had manipulated the Berringer-Dyce relationship to the point where they would shortly come nose to nose and would stir up enough trouble to warrant the strong hand of the Eagle Pass Council. Run, of course—behind the scenes to be sure—by the strong man.

He was sorry not to have been able to go out to his shooting place, with its targets and privacy, but it was also necessary to practice the draw, the turn, to study himself in the big mirror. And he had to admit that the figure he saw there did look impressive. And he had improved. He was very sure of that.

As he stepped out of his house on his way to his breakfast at the Last Stop Café, he heard his first firecracker. He smiled, thinking what a fine thing the Fourth was. Everyone together, paying fealty to their country, their state or territory, their town.

As he walked down the nearly deserted street, nodding at the aged swamper who was sweeping the boardwalk outside Two-Ton Priscilla's place, he felt the strength and sureness of his step, the irrevocability of his plan. Everything had been taken care of. All that awaited now was its execution. Dyce and Berringer, the submission of the town, and the silencing, possibly the elimination, of Mr. John Slocum.

Yes, indeed, a beautiful morning. And, as another firecracker went off, this time closer, he smiled, thinking how that evening or at any rate, as soon as all the hard action was done with, he would return to the pursuit that had been interrupted by all this activity: the pursuit of that lovely blond creature with the charming blue eyes who had regarded him with such disdain that he had decided on the spot that he had to have her. She was the newest acquisition in that stable of Two-Ton Priscilla Handles, and Priscilla had assured him that she was following her instructions in keeping an eye on the man Slocum.

The midafternoon sun was literally burning through his clothing as Slocum sat the Appaloosa just about halfway between Eagle Pass and Crazy Wolf Crossing. He had chosen the place carefully, sure that it would be from here that what he expected would begin. Right now he was watching the little cloud of dust growing bigger.

At first it had only been a spot on the horizon, but now it was nearer, and it had become long and narrow, rising out of the hard, hot earth, enveloping everything under it, moving slowly toward Slocum, now with a rumbling roar.

Then, all at once, near it a rifle cracked and then another, followed by a third. As Slocum watched, he saw the cloud of dust explode into a hundred parts, re-forming almost instantly into an enormous mass, a thundering avalanche, the sound of which increased with every pounding hoof.

Slocum didn't hesitate. His heels dug into his horse's flanks, and it leapt forward to meet the oncoming mass of bovine fear and fury.

Through the dust Slocum could see the longhorns, more than two thousand stampeding beasts, crazy with sudden terror. Their thundering hooves made the earth tremble beneath them.

He rode in a direct line for the center of the stampede, the dust choking him, burning his eyes, cutting into his face like tiny blades. The Appaloosa knew his work. He turned quickly when they reached the cattle, slowing his pace to keep only a jump ahead of them, thus allowing Slocum to lash their faces with his short-handled whip.

The attack made the leaders turn slightly and alter their course as Slocum drove at them, striking heavily and swiftly and without letup, until they had turned completely around, and the other beeves followed, turning into a milling mass.

Now the swing riders of the herd, who hadn't been

able to reach the leaders, surrounded the cattle, keeping them milling around until, as swiftly as it had started, the stampede was finished, and the cattle were grazing peacefully, as though nothing at all had happened.

The bony, leather-necked man who rode up to him now on the big dun gelding had a glint in his eye, and though Slocum had never seen him before, he knew who he was.

"Reckon as how that there's about the slickest I ever seen a stampede turned back. I got a notion your name is Slocum."

"I got a notion yours is Dyce."

Morgan Dyce nodded. "I got my men chasing those sons of bitches what started the stampede, but they don't have much chance of catchin' them. The buggers took off directly the animals started their run. They'll be to hell and gone by now."

"You're heading for town."

"I am. Ride along, if you've a mind to, we can chin."

"Good enough," Slocum said, reining the Appaloosa so he fell in beside the cattleman. "I would suggest you skirt the town."

"I was told the best way is to go straight through. Saves a lot of time. A lot, I was tolt."

"Excepting, it's the Fourth of July."

"What's that to do with it? They've had their chance, and they lost out. You sayin' they'll try again?"

"I know they will. Fourth of July means firecrackers. How do you figure your stock will handle that kind of gunfire?"

Something that looked like a grin appeared on the rancher's lined face. "Good enough then. You lead the way."

At that point, E. T. Crimmins appeared, nodding to Slocum. "That was real neat," the ramrod said. "Name's Crimmins."

"Slocum here says it's best to not go through the town like Berringer told us, but to go around," Dyce said to E.T.

"Makes sense, on account of I heerd it's the Fourth of July."

"How'd you know that?" his boss asked, suddenly suspicious that he hadn't been told.

"Heard him say it," E.T. explained and wiped his hand over his face.

"You got big ears," said Morgan Dyce with a sour grin. "Now tell me what we're gonna do about whoever started that stampede. We'll be out here a while gentlin' them down a touch more. Tell me. You think it was Berringer?"

They were riding three abreast now and the rancher spat over the top of his horse's head, narrowly missing an ear, which the animal twitched.

"I don't think it was Berringer," Slocum said, cutting in. "I don't think Berringer's working against you, Dyce."

"I take it you know him, else you wouldn't be talkin' that way."

"I have talked with him," Slocum said. "I think somebody else has been stirring the pot 'tween the two of you. Not that it's any of my business, because it isn't. Except so far as the Mulrooneys go. I'm workin' for them—sort of."

"Jesus—" said the rancher, and he reached up with his forefinger to pick something out of his back teeth. "What you're saying is that whoever's slickered this here stampede is the one and the same bin tryin' to get me and Berringer 'gainst ourselves. Course, that wasn't much but pretty easy in the first place," he added. "Even so, I do believe you could be talkin' about a gent named Glen Denning."

"Yeah." Slocum nodded. "Glendenning."

The foreman of the Double Back D cut his eye fast at his boss and said, "The name is one word, Morgan. Glendenning."

"I don't give a royal shit if it's five words. The son of a bitch is into too much of everything around here. All I hear is that name. Who and what is he, and why is he here? The son of a bitch sounds like he's with the railroad or somethin'."

"That's about the size of it," Slocum said. "My reading is he's out for himself, but speaking for what they call the Eagle Pass Council, or what's going to be the council after the election."

"Election? When the hell is that?" Dyce asked.

"Today," said his foreman.

"Good enough." Dyce nodded his head as though in agreement with something he was thinking.

"What d'you mean by that?" E.T. asked, but the boss of the Double Back D didn't say another word all the way in to town.

He heard the firecrackers as soon as he reached the livery at the end of Main Street. The Appaloosa responded by spooking a little, more pretense actually, since he was more than likely figuring on some oats. That was how Slocum read it as he dismounted and led the horse into the gloomy interior.

"Come in for the cellybration, did ya?" said the voice coming out of the dark.

"Yup. How're things going?"

"Good enough. They had the election. The council won it."

"Same people still in, eh?"

"That's the size of it." The raspy voice now came closer as the rangy figure appeared out of the gloom, along with the smell of horse manure and leather.

"Town's gonna wear itself out," the old hostler said. "I figger everybody's drunk about everythin' and only thing left is to sleep it off." He leaned in the direction of the big doorway, through which could be seen the fading light of the sky.

Slocum handed him money. "I do him myself as a rule."

"That I know, mister. But you best be gettin' on uptown. They is expectin' you." And his voice lowered on these last words so that Slocum could barely hear him.

"Whereabouts?"

"Two-Ton's place likely. Dunno for sure. But I seen certain people goin' in there."

"You say the council is all elected now?"

The hostler, whose name was Sigurd, nodded. He was a tall, lean, bent old man who appeared to be pretty much stove up. Slocum figured the old boy was a former bronc stomper who'd waited too long to retire. Of course, Slocum reflected, who didn't wait too long? It was part of the trade to keep going till you couldn't anymore.

"Drink?" Sigurd said.

"Join you."

They were in the tack room now and the bottle was within easy reach, plus two well worn mugs. That is, they were scarred and filthy, though perhaps slightly cleaner after Sigurd wiped them with his hands.

"Not bad," Slocum said, knocking his drink back.

" 'Nother?"

"No. That'll do her."

"C'mon. It's the Fourth!"

Slocum measured him then. "You were told to get me drunk. That it?"

The hostler nodded. Then, swiftly, he poured another drink for himself as well as for his guest. But before Slocum could protest, Sigurd poured the drink from Slocum's mug into his own, and he said in a fairly loud voice, "To us, by God!" And clinked the two mugs together as though they were having another toast.

Slocum, too, had heard their company. He saw Sigurd's eyes go up toward the loft, and he nodded.

"Well, I'll be heading for Two-Ton Priscilla's," he said.

The hostler nodded, and poured himself another drink.

"You take care of the Appaloosa," he said to the hostler.

"Sure will. An' you take care yerself, mister," the stableman said, his eyes lifting to the ceiling of the tack room, which was directly beneath the hayloft. His voice was almost a whisper. "You know the back way in? You got to go into that back alley right outside Doc Linus's office, then around the corner. The back door is locked, as a rule. But you can jimmy it. You got something? A knife?"

Slocum nodded. "The Appaloosa," he said. "Leave his rigging on." And he was gone.

It was dark outside now, and Slocum figured he'd maybe slipped out without the man in the loft knowing, for he heard Sigurd talking as though he was still in the livery, which would give him a little time.

He knew his way and in only a few minutes was at the back of Doc Linus's office. It crossed his mind to go in and see Doc, but he dropped it, figuring it would only eat up time, and thus kill any surprise he might use to his advantage, especially since whoever had been in the loft might report his presence in town.

All this speculation came to nothing in the next moment, as he saw the shadowy figure at the back of the house.

"Ho—" It was Doc, taking a leak. "That you, my friend?"

"It's me," Slocum said. "That's it."

Both had spoken in a low tone.

"Come inside. I had better bring you up on what's going on around here."

Without a word, Slocum followed him into his office, watched as Linus locked the door behind them, and made sure the shades were covering the windows. The coal oil lamp threw both their shadows on the walls of the room as they found their chairs and sat facing each other.

"I heard there was a stampede of the Double Back herd," Doc said.

"Where'd you hear that?"

"It's all over town by now. I heard it in Priscilla's place. Somebody said Indians, somebody else said Berringer had lit it. Take your pick." He paused, studying Slocum, who remained silent. "Or, I see you're thinking what I'm thinking, my friend."

Slocum nodded. "I was there," he said. "Sure, I didn't see how it started, but it wasn't Indians. There was rifle fire. Spencers. The tribes don't have guns, and for sure not Spencers. Besides, why would they want to stampede the herd?"

"Then what about Berringer?" Linus asked.

"I don't believe it was him. I had a good talk with Berringer. He is a lot of things, but he isn't dumb."

"That's it. Sure," said Doc, studying it with his brows knit. "That leaves the—" He let it hang.

"It leaves the bunch who are represented by Glendenning," Slocum said. "It leaves Glendenning."

"And the council." And then he looked directly at Slocum, his eyes wide open in surprise, and he pointed his finger at himself. "That leaves me! Me, the council. Shit!"

"You're in a good position," Slocum told him, holding out his palm to calm him.

"Hah! Sure!"

"Yes, sure. This thing is going to bust wide open, and somebody will be very much needed to handle things, to pick up all the loose strings. To stop the stampede. Because there will be a stampede. A human stampede, and somebody had better be there who knows what he's doing and hasn't got his hand in everybody else's pockets."

"You think it's ready to bust?"

"It has got to."

"Are you figuring to go over to Two-Ton's place, or for the matter of that, any other saloon, bar, dancing hall, or house of entertainment? Or even to your room at the Longhorn? Well, you had better not."

"You're telling me there's a greeting committee to celebrate my return to Eagle Pass?"

"I am. You are a target, my friend. But I guess you know that."

"What do you recommend as a start?" Slocum asked with a quiet grin. "Where would you say they are most concentrated?"

"I'd guess Two-Ton's. I've supposedly got a patient to tend to, so I'm free of whatever the plan is. But I do know that Glendenning's got all his boys out. What it is he has in mind, I can't say. But my guess is that at this stage he might very well try to get you." He stopped suddenly, his face much more serious now as he seemed to realize the importance of what he'd been saying. "Look, John. I can hide you out till you can get out of here."

But Slocum was already shaking his head slowly from side to side. "That's no good. Look, next thing he'll move in on the Mulrooneys, and he's for sure going to try again to pit Dyce against Berringer, and maybe even get the army in here. They'll do what he wants, on account of it'll come from back East. You know how those things work."

"I do. I do. An Indian uprising, outlaws on the trail, a town without protection, terrified of the famous gunman and all that! But you can't beat them all by yourself. You can't owe that much to Clyde Mulrooney!"

Linus stopped suddenly, noticing how quiet his companion was. A silence fell into the room now. Slocum sat in his chair without moving. A moment passed. Another. Slocum hadn't made an answer to what Linus had said, though Doc wasn't actually expecting an answer, but some kind of response would have certainly eased the moment. Slocum was looking at him, and Doc finally had to look away.

It was Slocum who finally broke it. His voice had a tone that Doc Linus had not heard in it before. "No, you're right. I don't owe that much to Clyde Mulrooney. I owe it to myself."

He stood up, gave a nod, and started to the door. But in the next split second he had spun on his heel, drawn his Colt, and had Doc Linus covered.

But Sophe Linus had already dropped the gun he had pulled from inside his shirt. It hit the floor and skidded an inch or so.

"I can't do it," he said, and his voice was shaking.

"That's what I know," Slocum said, holstering the Colt. "But I wanted you to know it. You're not a killer. Maybe that's where Glendenning made his big mistake, thinking you were."

There were tears standing in Doc's eyes as he said, "He had me thinking I was. Or, I don't know. I guess I had begun to think that way already. I don't know." Suddenly, standing there he covered his face with his hands. "How long did you know?" he asked, speaking through his fingers, and then dropping his hands to his sides.

"Mostly right now I'd say, but some of it before."

"You're a sharp man, John Slocum."

"You told me too much about where the men were staked out. It had to be you were trying to get me off my guard."

"Hunh."

"You're no gunman, Sophocles. You'd better stick to Shakespeare." He looked over at Hamlet, the cat, who had just moved silently into the room and was seated on his haunches, licking a paw.

"See, that's how those buggers like Glendenning work. They get something on a man, and then they kill him by degrees."

"By God, that's for sure. But I don't care any more. I am not a killer. I did what I thought was right for— for her—Catherine—"

"I know," Slocum said. "The three of us know it."

And reaching down, he turned the key to unlock the door.

"The three! You and me and Glendenning know it. Yes."

"No," Slocum said as he opened the door. "You and me and Hamlet."

With a nod he was gone.

Sometimes the biggest surprise can be the smallest, the simplest. Slocum understood this. Instead of heading directly for the obvious, he decided to visit two of the other saloons before Two-Ton's. Thus, he checked in at Three-Finger Harold's and at the Everlasting before heading for the place where he had learned from Linus that Glendenning and his coterie were playing cards. By then he knew that the word had traveled well ahead of him; and he decided to keep the boys waiting. Thus, he returned to the livery and, avoiding Sigurd the hostler, found a spot in the now deserted loft and waited. He waited a good while, figuring the time when things in Two-Ton's place would be close to the boil, and then he climbed down and, making sure Sigurd wasn't around, made his way to the Premier Saloon Drinking and Eating Emporium. He was hoping that Nellie was well out of it. As for Linus, he didn't give him a thought.

As he approached the end of the street and Skintown, he wondered if they had men hidden outside, whether the place was crowded, and where Glendenning and his council might actually be.

The barroom was unusually silent, not at all like a Fourth of July night, and especially at a time of election, but he knew the reason. He was the reason. Besides, the election, he'd learned, had been a foregone conclusion. The council had swept into office as everyone had expected.

When he stepped through the swinging doors, he saw the men at the bar: two men packing hardware and some men he'd seen hanging around town the last time he'd been in the bar. All in all, he spotted four armed hard cases, with a couple of others who were the type who could go either way. He wondered if any of the tough boys were Berringer men. There was no sign of Glendenning or the council. Other than the half dozen men and the bartender, the place was unusually empty. And as he came in, two of the men departed, trying to conceal their haste. That left the four hard cases. They had spread themselves so that each one was now covering a corner of the room. The balcony, he noted through the mirror, was empty.

A man now entered from the back door and walked slowly and none too steadily to the bar. Slapping down a silver dollar onto the mahogany, he demanded another drink.

"Maybe take it slow, Tyrone," the bartender said, his eyes looking carefully at Slocum and the four gunmen.

"Take it easy, ye sez! A Tyrone don't never take it easy, by God!" And he slammed the palm of his hand down on the bar. "By God, I feed the best drink in the whole wurrld to this here crazy country and I got no need to be told to take it easy. Who the hell you take me fer!" He suddenly reeled back from the bar and began punching the air around him. "I'm the Tyrone, I am! Stonehead Tyrone Tyrone! I pack the whiskey an' I kiss the girls, I pinch their arses, and I pull their curls!" And he broke into a heavy, soaking laughter, wheezing, coughing, spitting, and staggering about the floor. "I never tolt yez, but I once challenged Sullivan himsilf, I did. For the title, by Jesus! But he wouldn't take me up on it. Scared, he was. Sullivan, the champion, he was scared of Stonehead Tyrone Tyrone! How you like that!"

Suddenly, as he began boxing the air and trying his fancy footwork, he kicked the cuspidor that was standing against the bar and almost fell.

At this point, the bartender came over to Slocum, who was standing at the end farthest from any of the four gunmen, though still within gun range.

"Mr. Glendenning wants to see you. He's in the back room."

"Tell him he can come out here if he wants to see me. And tell those four clowns holding up those corners to get out of here, or I'll sic Mr. Tyrone on them."

"*The* Tyrone, it is, goddamn ye. *The* Tyrone!"

"You've got sharp ears for a drinking man," Slocum said with a grin. "I'll bet you're not as sloshed as you're making out."

"Fuck yoursilf!"

"Don't know how. Maybe someday someone will show us poor mortals how to fuck ourselves, but right now—" He shrugged.

At that point a man entered the saloon and started toward the far end of the bar. He was wearing a brace of six-guns. And almost on his heels a second gunman entered and walked to the opposite end of the bar; he was also armed with two holstered guns.

Suddenly Slocum flicked his eyes to the balcony. He was sure something or someone had moved; but now there was nothing in sight. Fleetingly he thought of Nellie and wondered if she'd been moving about, maybe trying to warn him. Too late for that. He was in the middle of it. But that was his style.

He knew there were enough of them to pick him off, sooner or later, but he knew, too, that in certain cases the code, such as it was, demanded some kind of confrontation. And it was just this, of course, that was building right now.

Now, one of the gunmen who had just come in and was at the far end of the bar started to walk slowly toward Slocum.

"That's a nice looking gun you got there, mister. Want to sell it?"

Slocum didn't answer.

"I ast you a question, mister."

"Well, by damn, mebbe he didn't hear ye," suddenly snapped Tyrone Tyrone, reeling out from the bar rail that had offered him the support he obviously needed.

"Shut up, old man!"

Slocum saw that the four men who had been standing in the corners of the room had now moved in closer toward the bar, making an arch just outside the two who had just entered.

By now the man who had made the offer to buy Slocum's gun was standing right in front of him. There was a sneer on his face, but Slocum didn't appear to be looking at him; his eyes were on the second gunman who had moved along the bar, closer to where the tableau of Slocum, the gunman, and Stonehead Tyrone had formed. It was clear to Slocum that Tyrone was an unexpected part of the scene. The man was really drunk and could hardly stand. But he kept talking a streak, about the old days of the bare-knuckle prize ring and what he was like when he challenged Yankee Sullivan, the champion.

Slocum had decided that the best thing he could do

would be to make use of the old boy. Suddenly he grabbed Tyrone's arm and shoved him against one of the pair of gunmen, and at the same time drew one of the other tough's guns and slammed it into his face. Then he brought the barrel of the gun down on the head of the first gunman, buffaloing him to the floor.

He dropped down just in time as a barrage of bullets came from the corners of the room, none of which hit him. For they had all been caught by surprise.

He crawled behind the bar where the barman was hiding, spotted one of the remaining four moving, and shot him in the chest.

Somebody was shouting, "Stop it! Stop it!"

It took Slocum a moment to realize it had to be the man who had just now entered the bar. And he knew from descriptions he had heard that it was Glendenning. The firing ceased as quickly as it had started.

"You men get out of here! Take them with you!" He nodded at the fallen gladiators. And then he swung on the ashen-faced barman. "And get this place cleaned up!"

But to Slocum's surprise, the bartender had more courage than he had shown until that moment. He said, "Where is Miss Priscilla? It's from her I take me orders."

Before the astounded Glendenning could reply to this insolence, Stonehead Tyrone Tyrone burst into raucous laughter. "By jiminy! He's from the auld sod, he is! You hear him, Mr. Denning! He don't take no orders from a greener, by Harry!" And then he stopped suddenly and stared at Slocum. "Holy Mother of God! Did ye ever see a man move that fast, and handle himsilf like it!" And he started to dance a jig, but kicked the cuspidor again and fell.

It was in that split second that Slocum saw something on the balcony and he heard a woman's voice. It was all too quick to register, for at the same time he saw Tyrone Tyrone move on the floor and he kicked the gun out of his hand, then, twisting, Slocum saw Glendenning in the mirror with the gun in his hand. Slocum moved; rather something—some kind of lightning inside him—moved, people later said. And the gun fell from Glendenning's smashed hand.

"Ye should of killed the son of a bitch!" screamed Stonehead from the floor.

And then a single shot rang ran out, and, turning, Slocum saw the girl who had been on the balcony now running up to where they were standing. She was holding the derringer; he remembered seeing it in her handbag.

He had holstered his own gun, and now he reached down and picked up the gun that Glendenning had dropped as he fell dead to the floor.

The girl was standing there shaking, her eyes staring down at the man she had killed.

"Nellie—" Slocum reached over and put his arm around her.

"He was going to shoot you," she said. "The son of a bitch—"

"You were working for him."

She nodded. "I was. But I—I told him no after, after I—we—" And suddenly she was crying and hardly able to stand on her feet.

At this point Doc Linus, Homer Content, Cal Phobis, and Ludlow Franks entered the room.

Doc said, "Mr. Slocum, will you please act as deputy sheriff for this town until we can get somebody permanent?"

The four council members were standing right in front of him now as he broke open his gun and reloaded.

"If you don't take too long," Slocum said, "I won't take too long to make up my mind. That satisfy you gentlemen?"

And taking Nellie by the arm he led her out of the room and upstairs to the balcony.

"You're all right now," he said as she sat down on the bed.

She nodded. "I am. He had something on me, but he outsmarted himself, I guess."

At that point they heard a grunt as the door was pushed open.

"Don't you believe in knocking?" Slocum said as Two-Ton Priscilla ambled in. "Where have you been?"

Two-Ton had walked to the dresser and was looking at herself in the mirror. "I never knock when I think there might be some action I could check on."

"Where were you during all the excitement?" Slocum asked again.

She was still looking at herself in the mirror, turning her head this way and that, touching her hair. "Taking care of my toilette and minding my own business. Now you—" And she turned suddenly to face Nellie who was sitting beside Slocum on her bed. And Slocum could feel her tighten as Two-Ton bore down on her.

"I am in need of a manager for this place. And I am going to let you accept the job."

There was a moment of stunned silence.

"But—but—" The girl was all but stammering in her surprise.

"You'll take a small percentage if you do a good job. Otherwise, out on your behind."

All the time she had been talking, she was dabbing at

her hair, turning her head to study herself from various angles.

Slocum laughed as he stood up. "That is the best news I've heard in this good while," he said. "Congratulations!" He leaned down and kissed Nellie on the cheek.

"Say, where you goin'?"

"I'd like to stay, but I've got some business."

"You'll come back?" Nellie was leaning forward, sitting on the very edge of the bed now. "You're not leaving forever."

"So long," he said. And he was gone—across the landing and down the stairs.

He didn't like leaving her like that; he really didn't. There was for sure something special about the girl. But now at the same time he realized there was something that had been bothering him, something that he wasn't satisfied with. Like something undone, not finished. But what?

Just in time he remembered for they were both at the bar where they had been when he'd first come in that day. The two Morgan Dyce men, with their hardware and their tough sneers. He remembered their names now: Honniger and Deltus. Yes, why had they left the scene so abruptly? And now he knew; they'd been working for Glendenning actually, and had been planted on Dyce. Well, Glendenning was dead now, so— But that inner voice that had kept him alive in the past was nagging inaudibly at him now.

"Well, here's the former fastest gun in the West," said the taller of the two as he drew and Slocum shot him in the guts; then Slocum shot his companion between the eyes before he'd gotten his gun even halfway out of his holster.

"Holy Mother of God," whispered Stonehead Tyrone Tyrone, the whiskey wagon tycoon and former heavyweight championship challenger as he stood almost invisible in the deep shadow furnished by the corner of Two-Ton Priscilla Handles's saloon.

Slocum stood looking down at the dead men: Deltus and Honniger. He still didn't know which was which. And as he turned and walked away, he really didn't think that it mattered.

What concerned him now was only one thing. And as soon as he reached the livery where the Appaloosa was waiting for him, he was on his way.

Sure, he missed Nellie. Sure, she was a terrific partner. But he was a man who liked to take his time in deciding on relationships and sometimes those decisions came real fast, and sometimes they took forever. There was no telling. The best relationship of course and without any argument was very easy to tell. It was the one that you were engaged in at the moment.

And not very long after those heavy reflections, he remembered what he'd thought and knew how absolutely true it was as he looked down into the soft, endlessly deep eyes of Miss Alison Mulrooney while they rode each other delightfully to the climax of their first pleasure that evening.

Waking during the night, Slocum found the girl also awake beside him, her naked body entwined with his.

"Can't you sleep?" he asked.

"I don't want to. I want to be with you."

"I think that's a real good idea."

"Can I ask you something?"

"Why not?"

"Promise not to get mad at me?"

"I promise. But I know what you're going to ask."

"How do you know?"

"I just do."

"So, what am I going to ask you?"

"Which person I've liked best that I've had intimate relations with."

"You beast! How did you know I was going to ask that?"

"I dunno. Just did. Are you mad?"

"Of course not."

A short moment of silence.

"So tell. Which? Or maybe it's too difficult a question."

"Oh no. It's not difficult. It's easy as pie."

"Then tell."

"Well—"

"The truth now."

"Of course!"

"Who?"

"Why, you."

"Me?" She raised up on an elbow and her nipple sprang to his lips.

"Of course!"

"But why 'of course'?"

"Because you're the person I'm with, that's why. Miss, didn't you learn anything in school?"